Nothing Left ı ....

Rachel Taylor

She had always held very strong opinions, but was never really an activist. She paid very close attention to the issues, and was outspoken, but never considered running for office. She was pro-choice and anti-gun, she wanted to save the environment and gay marriage, but never thought of saving the world. She had gone to the women's march proudly, daughter by her side, counting herself among the masses that were protesting this new reality. Yet she never thought that her singular voice carried much weight. She had said many times that all they needed was someone with nothing left to lose….

1

She sunk into the chair, it seemed like it was swallowing her whole. His hand squeezing hers tightly, the only thing keeping her from drowning as the room swirled around her. She kept trying to focus on the face across the desk, on the voice coming out of it's mouth, but the harder she tried the further away it became. The heartbeat pounding in her ears was drowning out his questions and the answers were like listening to the WHAH WHAH from Charlie Brown's teacher. For some reason this caused a chuckle to bubble up from her throat, but all that emerged was a moan, and she felt she must be going mad. The room became blurry; the bright light from the huge windows intensifying to a complete whiteout, and she briefly thought that this must be what it feels like to stand on the sun. Brighter and brighter the light, and lighter and lighter her head became until she was sure it would pop like a balloon as she felt herself slipping into unconsciousness.

She woke up in his arms unsure of where she was and for a split second she smiled; relieved to be in her own bed and waking from the nightmare. The room came slowly into focus and as he stroked her hair she realized that there was no waking up from this. He tried to feign a smile, but the tears in his eyes didn't lie, and as he kissed her knuckles one slid down his face and lingered on the tip of his nose before it fell silently onto the blanket. No treatment options. No cure. No warning. For the first time in her life, she was one in a million and all at once everything looked different. She glanced around the room, her gaze falling on the pictures of her family arranged on her dresser. How she loved that picture of her dad, her with her brothers and sisters by the lake, her aunts, her babies. She could feel the warm sting of tears as she looked at the curtains she had chosen to compliment the dust ruffle that he was sure they didn't need, and the perfect pillow she had chosen for the armchair they'd had since their very first apartment. It wasn't until she looked down at her own hands that the tears fell fast and furious. How many more times would she look at them? How many more times would they make a dinner, open a door, wipe her ass? Everything looked different in the shadow of the end. By all estimations she would be gone within a year, and she would take with her every dream they'd ever had. It would all be over before that long awaited, much saved for trip to Europe or that next class reunion. Those hands would most likely not hold that first grand baby or help their daughter into her wedding dress. Instead they would soon be holding a pen, figuring out how to write letters of goodbye.

The next few weeks were spent comforting others and trying to forget that there were only a mere 24 hours in every day. It was hard to tell where one stage of grief ended and the next began because she seemed to be experiencing them simultaneously. Hours and minutes normally taken for granted became a precious commodity and family stories became the stuff of legend as they were told and retold. She noticed that she would never hear the word goodbye quite the same way again, the finality of it clinked dully in her soul like a coin being dropped in a can. The whole world looked different at the ass end of a terminal diagnosis; don't sweat the small stuff became the understatement of the century. The bright side was that everything tasted better, and dying had quieted the guilt that came with cellulite. She thought glibly how she would never have to diet again and how convenient it was that her concerns about her aging looks were now a thing of the past. Her requests were never denied her and the limited amount of time that was left now meant she could finally live like no one was watching, only to realize that everyone was.

When it finally dawned on her that she was leaving silently and in a hurry without ever having made a difference, it was like hearing the words "I'm so sorry" echo in her ears all over again. It was as if she were standing in a house filled with doors but chose to climb unnoticed out the bathroom window. There was supposed to be more. She'd always thought that there would be more. Wasn't there supposed to be more? A life that had been lived so loudly and with no apologies was now fizzling out with barely a whisper. This world wasn't any better off for her having lived, she was just another cog in the wheel and her existence had meant nothing. She wasn't leaving this world anything. No beautiful piece of art or work or literature, no grand gesture or words of wisdom. She had never healed the sick or won the Nobel Peace Prize. Shit, she had never even been to college. A wife and a mother was all she'd ever been, and now it was all she would ever be.

On most days she dangled between the depths of despair and callous resignation, never seeming to find any middle ground. The emotions usually came in waves and she had stopped accepting the phone calls and visits because sometimes the jealousy of knowing they would all move on with their lives when they moved beyond her driveway was too much to bear. Their pity made her more nauseous than the meds, and she could see it in their eyes; the wonder if this was the last time they'd see her without her head on a satin pillow. They tried to hide it, but they were always taking that mental snapshot; the one they would tell everyone about when it was all over. Some days were better than others and on her less than stellar ones, lying in bed watching the world fall apart seemed the best form of commiseration. He still needed to go to work while he could, and she had forbidden the kids to hover after it was clear that they could not keep her company without holding a box of Kleenex. The only soap she had watched had been canceled years ago when there was no time or reason to lie in bed all day taking solace in the fact that every character's life was so much more desperate than her own. Instead she switched constantly between sitcom episodes she had seen a thousand times, cooking shows and the news. There were 12 channels of nothing but news, and the news was never good. She wondered day after day what fresh hell her grand baby would endure and how unfair it was that she would not be there to protect her only son's little one. It was way too early to know the baby's gender and part of her almost didn't want to know, as her mind was now in the habit of breaking her heart with all the things she could not control. Whether a girl or boy, she could think of a thousand things that she would be missing, she didn't need to assign a sex and make the heartbreak gender specific.

2

Lying in bed watching the news immediately catapulted her back into the fog of disbelief that engulfed her when the world came crashing down one Tuesday in November. The fear and complete sense of helplessness shook her to her very core and until recently it was as near to being in a state of shock as she had ever been. She remembered that she stayed up that whole night and cried, watching the results roll in one after another; flinching at every win like she had touched a hot stove. It was the worst day of her life until the day she found out that she might not last to see how it would all end. When he woke up the next morning and saw her still awake; eyes swollen, he just hugged her and said, " Cry all you want today, because tomorrow, we fight."

Right up until that very night, no one thought he could get elected. He himself certainly didn't believe anyone would elect him. A textbook sociopath with a blatant narcissistic personality disorder and the heir to a flavored seltzer water empire, he started a run for the highest office in the country solely for the attention. The last thing he wanted to do was to be bothered with the tedious duties of running a country, and when he began his campaign; which now seemed an eternity ago, all he really ever wanted was to be the center of the Universe. Even he didn't realize how this exercise in narcissism would fuel that desire, and where it would lead. Standing in front of the masses that filled his endless rallies, he spewed untruths and hurled insults, each one louder and more outrageous than the one before, because the sound of his own voice seemed to arouse him. He loved the praise, but he FED off the criticism of his opposition, and the chanting of his name left track marks on his arm. He was neither charming nor handsome nor charismatic. He was only one thing and one thing only. He was DIFFERENT. Completely different than all who had come before him and that was enough. In a dry, brittle political climate on the brink of combustion, one tiny match was more than enough. He incited riots, mocked the disabled, called for the death of his opponent, and still his minions, followed their pied piper right off a cliff, all the while cheering the end of the career politician. Every racist remark, every misogynistic comment was excused because he was a businessman who would learn presidential etiquette as he went along. When he was proven to be a sexual predator, normally rational people turned their heads. He didn't care that the country was divided and imploding, he only cared that he had caused it. More to the point, he was PROUD that he had caused it. The experiment had failed. He had won, and the world was different now.

Almost immediately the change began. The war on women, minorities and a free press was the most evident and he would shake his head yes while his mouth said no. He declared journalists enemies of the state as he cozied up to tyrants and alienated allies. He lied about everything from the size of the crowd at his inauguration, to his relationship with one of the world's most powerful dictators. He declared war on the environment and education, and spoke at a third grade level. One by one, rights that had been taken for granted for generations were rescinded in the name of a God he most certainly did not believe in. The building of a wall was started "to protect" it's citizens, although it's citizens were now being locked in with the people they feared the most. It became acceptable to be a bigot. No longer were the racists hiding in the dark, hatred was growing right there in the sunlight. His never ending hate speech and constant diatribe about immigrants led to mass shootings and domestic terrorism. Friends and family became estranged; you were either for or against, and even those straddling the fence were viewed as the red headed stepchild by both sides. The number of people being treated for depression and anxiety skyrocketed, and the suicide rate was at an all time high. Most days it was devastation at worst and utter chaos at best.

Night after night they would watch slack jawed as the insanity of the day's events was displayed on the evening news. Everything from his oversized, ill fitting suits and overly coiffed comb over, to his orangutan orange spray tan screamed lunatic. Not a day went by that the anger towards those who chose to turn a blind eye didn't boil over. Still, she marched and protested and she protested and marched and she voted. When they lost the mid term elections to his party, it became clear that they would have to ride out his first term until they could vote him out of office. It could all be undone because after all, it was still a democracy, and the sane still outnumbered the insane. At least that's what they all told themselves.

Truth be told, for many, the world had become an alternate reality. It was now commonplace to be told that what was seen with eyes and heard by ears was not reality. The constant barrage of lies was meant to confuse his followers and wear down the resistance. Half of his cabinet was either under investigation or under arrest from anything from tax fraud and campaign violations, to sexual assault, to colluding with a foreign power to steal the election. It was impossible to keep track of who had been found guilty and who was standing trial, and worse still, none of it seemed to matter to his followers. They gobbled up the lies, swallowing them whole. They hit share on every social media post and couldn't be bothered to research facts. He was backed 100% by a political party that loathed him but who was counting on the dumbing down of the population to further their agenda.

It was exhausting and mentally draining to keep fighting with the hordes and to keep hope alive where none seemed possible. The world waited for outcomes of countless investigations, for him to be indicted, for the scourge to be lifted and for justice to prevail so that life could get back to normal, but there seemed to be no end in sight. He was a monster of mythical proportions. So much so that reading that he was a monster of mythical proportions would bring a shit eating grin to his face, after he asked someone what mythological meant, or made the definition up himself.

When the resistance failed to produce a candidate moderate enough to win over the followers, those that still had retained their sanity wondered aloud (but not too loudly) why no attempt had been made on his life. So many had lost their healthcare, their jobs and their homes that it was bizarre that no attempt had been made to end the country's suffering. Assassination attempts on previous presidents had been made for far less than the sins he was committing daily. No one even tried to step up to the plate when there was talk that he would try and convince his mostly corrupt Congress to suspend the next election. The most powerful country in the history of the world was being threatened with autocracy and no one blinked, because as was becoming the norm, that thought seemed completely unimaginable. The unimaginable now seemed a thing of the past because it had been proven time and time again in this alternate reality that nothing was impossible. The impossible had already been accomplished in so many ways and on so many levels that the memories of living in the country of her childhood were more like dreams.

It was unbelievable how much of a democracy could be undone while the country slept and every morning the world awoke and braced itself for the damage report. How many times had they said it couldn't get any worse, that people couldn't continue to believe the lies that became more outrageous every day. They wouldn't turn their backs on the freedoms that generations fought for; that their parents fought for. They wouldn't relegate their children to living under a dictatorship. Day after day she watched as the twelve news channels paraded experts and pundits past the television audiences who were constantly clamoring to hear someone tell them what they wanted to hear, or fight about what they didn't. Finally though after 7 long years the end of his reign was in sight. He could not serve another term, but so much damage had been done to the country that it would take years to recover if recovery was even possible. His followers and his policies would see to that.

Theirs was a nation divided almost to the brink of civil war, literally brother against brother. Soon enough though, they would be rid of him and that was the only chance they had of moving forward. The resistance had won these last mid term elections and a woman now stood third in line for his position. It was a thin victory though, as the patients continued to run the asylum.

3

On one of her particularly bad days, she was lying in bed, remote in hand, her sixteen year old terrier dutifully at her side. She had spent so many years dreading the loss of this animal, and now like everyone else, this sweet puppy that she always referred to as her "third child" would be outliving her. She was lost in thought when the all too familiar graphic took over the TV screen. BREAKING NEWS. She had seen it so often since "the change" that it almost didn't warrant being alarmed anymore. Everything everyday was alarming and sometimes it was just a matter of choosing your battles. How offended were you prepared to be today? Was a female senator being called "horse face" or was a foreign country being threatened with nuclear war? It didn't escape her that by threatening to blow a country off the map it made attacking a female's body or looks seemingly harmless in comparison. And with harmless came acceptable.

That's how this entire war on normalcy had been waged, by fear. Throughout history fear has always been the way to keep the masses in line.

The look on the news anchors face sent a shiver up her spine. It was obvious that he was trying to remain composed, but the fear behind his eyes made her sit up straight in bed. He was sitting all by himself at the news desk, his sleeves rolled up to his elbows. She knew this guy; this veteran anchor, and she liked him. He always looked disgusted and she'd caught him on numerous occasions rolling his eyes and shaking his head while trying desperately to act non-biased. She noticed his hair had gotten grayer these last few years. It was not a surprise that any self- respecting journalist had aged just trying desperately to keep up with the constant war on their profession and the truth. The phrase "coming unglued" jumped into her mind as she watched him struggling to keep it together as he delivered what would undoubtedly be the most important 90 seconds of his career. For the first time in weeks she wished she wasn't alone and she struggled to focus on what was being said. She turned up the volume and the dog stirred in her sleep, blissfully unaware of the importance of this single moment.

The anchor's words ran out of his mouth like they were being chased, and tripped over themselves as they hit the air. She was trying so hard to comprehend what he was saying that at first his urgency didn't make sense. A terrorist attack she thought, it's finally happened, he's started World War Three. Her mind raced to mentally locate her family and still stay calm enough to figure out what to do next. Slowly, she realized there were no tests of the emergency broadcast system, no alarms, no instruction ribbon running along the bottom of the screen. All at once she realized that this journalist was scared. Scared about what he was reporting, but even more so for his own personal safety. His eyes darted back and forth, not looking into the camera but through it; like he was trying to make out something on the other side.

A secret session of Congress. In the dead of night. A Coup. The end of the Constitution. Dictator. Civil war. Treason. His words were like machine gun fire; she was only getting bits of what he was saying and she was still processing the information, trying to piece it all together when two men came on screen. He held on to the sides of the desk, not giving up, shouting now. She was off the bed and standing in front of the set now, not realizing that her hands had traveled to her face and were covering her mouth. She watched as the two men grabbed him underneath the arms, one trying desperately to shut him up as they dragged him out of the studio. A woman off camera was screaming as the news cut abruptly to commercial and she was left staring at a male enhancement ad wondering if her meds caused hallucinations. She turned and saw the dog still sleeping soundly on the bed, and for a moment thought about crawling back underneath the covers to sleep off whatever delusions she had been experiencing. Instead, she picked up the remote and changed the channel. Every network was on a commercial break. Every. Single. One. Raising the shade on her bedroom window, she expected total chaos, but looking out onto the street she saw nothing amiss, nothing out of place. She picked up her cell phone and hit the "my love" contact thinking with a sickening feeling that she'd hit that button for so long she hadn't ever memorized the number. She had better memorize that number. He'd heard nothing about it. No chatter at the office, nothing on the radio. Convinced she had been dreaming, he told her that he loved her and to lie down. So she did.

4

She woke up as the purple glow of twilight filled her room and she tried to shake off the grogginess that comes with an afternoon nap. The dog was no longer next to her, and a feeling of safety washed over her when she saw that his car was in the driveway. What she had seen on TV, or what she THOUGHT she had seen seemed more like her imagination now after a deep sleep. As relieved as she was, she now worried that this was the start of a new symptom. She brushed her hair and pinched her cheeks hoping to give her husband some illusion of a wife healthier than the one he was suffering with and went downstairs.

He smiled when he saw her and she was in his arms before her feet hit the bottom step. These days it wasn't unusual for him to show an inordinate amount of affection. As his arms encircled her she could feel that there was more to it than the realization that the number of hugs he had left was dwindling. After 25 years of hugs, it was something that she just knew. He drew away from her and smiling or not, his brow was furrowed and that was never a good sign. He led her to the couch and handed her his phone. It was all over social media he told her. All of the posts were taken down as quickly as they were posted but people took screenshots and were texting them to family and friends. What she had seen was being reported on almost every news channel just like she had described it to him over the phone, and the president was calling it bogus news. Every government statement denied that what she had seen actually occurred, and the resistance was trying desperately to unravel the lies and get to the truth. What they did know regardless of his denial, was that a secret meeting of his cabinet had been called in the dead of night to discuss postponing the presidential election. The end game of course was to postpone the election long enough to secure the amount of votes needed to extend his term, so that he could remain in office. It was the first active step towards dictatorship by a desperate man realizing it had been discovered that the emperor was buck ass naked.

As they sat there in the living room surrounded by decades of memories that screamed their truth, they tried to decide what to do with all of the lies. What to do next was not a conversation that they ever thought they would have. Her death was not a conversation that they had ever thought they would have either, but at least over the years they had done what most couples do and played the "what if" game. What if you go, what if I go, what if you find someone else… blah, blah, blah, the kind of things that you can't help but discuss through years of ups and downs, nights of drinking and talking and lying naked in each other's arms. What to do when your government becomes a dictatorship? Not a discussion they'd ever had.

How they viewed today's events couldn't be more polar opposite. She instinctively wanted to run. Take the children and go now, before everything that was being denied came to fruition and this madman's henchmen came knocking door to door. He told her that he would not run. She had never heard her husband mention fighting a parking ticket let alone a civil war, but here he was telling her that he wanted to buy a gun. This passive, peace loving man she thought she knew better than herself, was saying that he would aggressively defend his country against real soldiers with real weapons. She suddenly realized that there was more than one way to be given a death sentence.

After talking for hours, they didn't come up with much more of a plan than deciding that they would take money out of accounts little by little as not to arouse suspicion. They called the kids, told them to do the same, keep their passports handy and wait and see what the next few days and weeks would bring. She was exhausted and ready to lie down again. There hadn't been much of an appetite lately and the day's events mixed with a new round of meds had made her downright queasy. She tried to convince him to let her fix him something, but he refused and was making himself eggs when she finally climbed the stairs to the sanctuary of their king sized bed.

5

The sunlight landed in the same spots in their bedroom as it had the day before assuring her that even the looming chaos couldn't change the trajectory of the sun. His side of the bed was still warm and she could smell the coffee brewing. She was thankful that her enjoyment of coffee hadn't changed. So many of her favorite things now tasted foreign to her, but coffee every morning tasted like normal. She lay there assessing what she called the first five. How her day would progress could usually be summed up within the first five minutes after her eyes opened. It was basically like taking a mental inventory of herself from head to toe, and she had learned her body's signs and which way they pointed. The first five told her that today was going to be a good day; a strong day, and she headed downstairs to get a good, strong cup of normal.

He was standing in the kitchen stirring his coffee and when he looked at her he knew the first five's verdict as well. He smiled and handed her his mug, grateful for a good day and a shared love of light and sweet. The events of the night before still hung in the room and neither of them wanted to ruin the promise of the day ahead with talk of what may be running amok beyond their four walls. They were avoiding their phones and the TV, scared of finding out just how bad things had gotten overnight, and not wanting to hear the damage report. They also knew that part of the plan was to scare the masses into denial and that every day was a good day to resist.

As they sat on the couch sipping coffee and looking at the beautiful day unfolding outside their window, he decided to play hooky. It was fall, and there always seemed to be such a short window of time where the leaves were in all of their glory and the weather was still mild. So few days like this to take advantage of she thought, so few days like this left to see. Most mornings she would have to force herself to even come downstairs to greet the day. More often than not, he would bring her coffee to her in her favorite mug, the one that said "shhh, there's whiskey in here". She loved it because when you tipped the mug it gave you the middle finger. She felt a wee sense of power most mornings flipping off the world under the covers with the shades drawn. Not today though. Today she was going to go out into the world and flip it off in person. She might even actually have that whiskey.

The morning air was crisp, and a light jacket was all that was needed as the afternoon had promised to turn warmer. Hand in hand they walked and every once in a while she would turn her head to look at his profile. She didn't know where she was going or what she could take with her, but she couldn't help memorizing every curve of his face, every hair in his goatee in case that was one of the bags she was allowed to board with. They were taking the long way downtown. The leaves would be so vibrant in the park and this route wouldn't take them past the cemetery, a fact they both realized but neither spoke about. She squeezed his hand and pressed her cheek into his shoulder as they strolled silently towards the park. Always a talker, she felt no need today for useless chatter. Something inside her whispered that they had been granted these few flawless hours as a gift not easily given, and not to blemish them with idle chit chat.

Their walk led them down their favorite trail; the one they had walked every year about this time with their little ones and then not so little ones. Dozens of Octobers spent watching deer and their new spring born fawns meander through the fallen leaves, and the squirrels hoard acorns for the upcoming harsh winter. They knew what color every tree on this path turned, and were always amazed by their fiery brilliance no matter how many years had gone by. She tried desperately to freeze this moment in time, tattooing the colors of the leaves emblazoned against this bright blue sky on her soul. She could remember being a child and the smell of the wet leaves as they covered her after a long awaited jump. For the rest of her life, that is what autumn would smell like.

For the rest of her life.

Lifting her face she closed her eyes, feeling the sun warm her face as the light danced across her closed eyelids. The leaves crunching under their feet sent a shiver up her spine. Once decorating the sky so bright they were blinding; now grounded and brittle, their time was up. The route they took snaked down by the river where they sat on a bench adorned with a plaque that said " In Memory of Sarah. We will NEVER stop loving you."and watched old men fishing from lawn chairs. Knowing her so well, he pulled a flask from the inside pocket of his jacket and they took turns sipping maple whiskey in the autumn sunshine.

6

The buzz from the whiskey made her feel fine, and she was suddenly hungrier than she'd been in what seemed like forever. Grinning from ear to ear he took her hand and pulled her gently off the bench, knowing that after weeks of not eating in solidarity, he was finally going to get his favorite burger at their favorite place downtown. The way things were going, he thought that he might even get a beer too.

The day was turning out to be one like they hadn't had in a long time, and as it turned out would never have again. Although not far from their minds, thanks to the whiskey, the sunshine and the first five, they were able to forget if even for a few fleeting moments, that another autumn would come without her. They may have even been able to forget the rest of the world around them if not for the crowd of people gathered outside the offices of their local representative. This particular politician had made it very clear in the last 7 years where his loyalties lie, and this wasn't the first time he had taken heat for it. They noticed now however, that the doors were locked, lights were off, and that man and his staff had gotten out of Dodge.

They saw that the crowd was growing and passed on the opposite side of the street continuing on to their favorite eatery in town. They'd been frequenting this mom and pop place since they had given up the city for small town life almost two decades ago. They'd not only made this their Friday family night place with the kids, but stumbled out of here countless Saturday nights after music and whiskey and laughter. They'd watched the owners retire and their kids take over. They'd given gifts to growing families and mourned when the patriarch passed leaving his wife of 60 years. They'd celebrated birthdays and anniversaries here; they found out they'd be grandparents here.

For a moment she had forgotten that everyone knew, and then she looked around at the faces looking up from their meals. Privacy was a casualty of small town life. She smiled awkwardly, silently giving every set of eyes permission to abandon the pity and continue eating their lunch. Thankfully it was lunchtime on a weekday and the patrons were at a minimum. Hugs from the owners saved her from the stares and they made a beeline to their usual table by the window overlooking the center of the town that they loved. From their vantage point inside the restaurant they could see that in a short period of time, the crowd of protesters outside the politician's offices had grown exponentially, and now were being joined by the opposition. Their own fears of the current political climate aside, neither one of them was alarmed by the size of the crowd, nor did they think it would turn into anything substantial. Protests in this new reality were not uncommon and most that took place in their little town ended with little more than raised voices and some name- calling. By the time their burgers and beers had arrived, so had the police.

They sat eating and watching, taking notice that a sense of concern was growing inside the restaurant, because outside things seemed to be getting more heated. They recognized many people in the crowd; on both sides. Many friends had been lost these last few years and that had stung at first. Later, the sting had been replaced by the realization that spending any amount of time with a person who supported the current government was a painful and frustrating experience. It was a deal breaker, a relationship ender. It was as though they had turned into another entity before your eyes; like watching your best friend or co worker turn into a werewolf, and you could never, ever see them the same way again. It was never NOT shocking to find out that someone you loved was not who you had always believed them to be.

It was interesting for them to be on the outside of this confrontation, experiencing it as bystanders and not participants. They were both itching to be an active part of the dissent; to be in the crowd sharing in the collective outrage. Mere months before she wouldn't have hesitated to get right in the middle of it all, but they both knew that was not a good idea in her current state. They had to be content to be involved passively, showing support and fighting the good fight from the sidelines; the Rosie the riveters of the resistance. As they finished up their lunches, discussing the best ways to stay involved given her current situation, a loud crash drew their attention back to the demonstration. A shrill car alarm followed, and from what they could make out as the melee got underway, a bicycle had been thrown through the windshield of a parked car.

7

Everyone in the restaurant was now at the large front window overlooking the square, abandoning their tables for a better look at the escalating conflict in what was usually a humdrum community. Realizing that everyone watching from the window knew everyone in that crowd, and everyone in that crowd knew each other, made the whole thing very personal. It wasn't hurling obscenities (or bicycles) at someone you'd never see again, or flipping off a stranger that cut you off in traffic. It was verbally abusing your next door neighbor's wife, and screaming in the face of your child's teacher or the receptionist at your dentist's office. It was finding out that your daughter's best friend's mom was not at all who you thought she was and now those kids will never play together again. Every witness to this vulgar display of frustration, whether involved or not would go on tomorrow to make decisions that affected their day to day based on whose beliefs they agreed with. Where they would bring their cars for repair, or get their keys made, or who would do their nails or hair would all be decided by whether or not they agreed with the political affiliations they saw displayed today. It was maddening, and even as they realized this about their neighbors, they knew that they would be guilty of this as well.

Every police officer in town (all five of them) was now in the square, obviously taken aback by the events unfolding as they tried to subdue an increasingly violent crowd. The decision had been made to stay right where they were until the mob had dispersed and things had been brought under control. A chant erupted from the angry protesters, low at first and then gaining strength as voices screamed out their fears in unison:

DEMOCRACY NOT AUTOCRACY they chanted, followed by shouts of NO KING. A couple of hundred people had congregated now, and what had started out as a calm gathering was now growing in anger and animosity as counter protestors provoked the once peaceful demonstrators. By the time the second grade teacher's husband had thrown the bicycle through the pharmacist's windshield, punches had already been thrown and normally passive people became unrecognizable as their faces twisted with rage.

The bicycle thrower was arrested first, followed by several others on both sides and little by little the officers were able to get the crowd to disperse. Inside the restaurant they were finishing up their beers, paying the bill and resisting the urge to insert their opinion into conversations at nearby tables. As much as they were wishing that they had stayed down by the river sipping whiskey instead of witnessing this disgusting symptom of their nation's demise, they knew that the only way to change anything was to keep their heads out of the sand.

They were anxious to continue on with what had started out as a perfect day, because soon she would be too exhausted to do much else and it would be time for another round of meds. They left the restaurant with more hugs and promises to return soon and headed back towards the house, passing the pharmacist who was now on the phone with her insurance company about her busted windshield. The bank was on their way home and especially after what they had just witnessed and knowing it was probably just the first of many more instances like this, the first of the with drawls was made. They realized that her health was enough reason not to raise any suspicions about pulling money out of their account, but nonetheless, they started with a small amount and would space the with drawls out as time would permit.

Continuing on towards home they held hands and had the all too frequent conversation about what had occurred outside the restaurant and the sadness that came with it. It was hard to watch, even harder to be a part of, but a necessity to save the country that they loved. Still, it seemed that with what was coming both politically and personally, they may need to distance themselves from the physical aspect of the resistance and they discussed possibly getting away for a while. The doctor's had made it a point to tell them that they should travel sooner than later and that once the bad days started to outnumber the good ones, they wouldn't want to be far from home. Where to go though? A nice quiet beach vacation where they could relax and be introspective? Or a more once in a lifetime trip doing things they'd always dreamed of? She told him that if there was ever a time to do once in a lifetime, it was now. It was bizarre for her to think that she would be making memories for someone else to enjoy and in the next few months she would leave everything that she had experienced and everything that she was with those that she loved for safekeeping. So once in a lifetime was the way to go, even if at this late hour it was more for all of them than for her.

8

She stood in the driveway staring at the house and contemplating this as he reached into the mailbox. Man, how she loved this house. She loved everything about it. She loved the feel of the grass under her bare feet in the summer, because she planted every blade of that grass. She loved how it's roof looked covered with snow in the winter; the lights from inside glowing out onto the street whispered cozy. Every plant, every flower put in place with her own two hands to bloom at just the perfect time every season. The backyard was their retreat. The large hedges offered all the privacy they needed from their neighbors without fences or walls. The fire pit she had built into the ground was her pride and joy, and it had seen many nights of music and good beer and bourbon, and maybe a time or two of lovemaking right there on the lawn beside it. Would she haunt this place she wondered? Would her spirit be able to leave the place where it felt most at peace? The tears nestled into the corners of her eyes and she willed them not to fall as he walked up beside her and squeezed her hand.

He got her the next round of meds and a large glass of water, grimacing as she turned on the television. They had avoided it long enough and she likened it to a train wreck; she didn't want to watch, but she couldn't look away. She sunk into the cushions wrapped in her favorite blanket, thinking it was chillier in this room than it had been on their walk, and wishing for an afternoon cup of coffee. Which channel, which channel she thought. Truth without spin, the facts ma'am, just the facts. She remembered how on their long drives he would always turn on the radio shows that spouted propaganda, saying that it was just as important to listen to the enemy. It kept you aware of how they were twisting the truth and alert to the direction of their attack. Right now though she was too tired to sift through the bullshit and all that she wanted was someone to tell her how bad today had actually gotten while she had been busy pretending it was just a normal day.

One thing was certain, changing the channel did not change the fact that in the era of social media, there were no secrets. What had happened the night before had gone global, and no cry of bogus news was going to change that. There were demonstrations and protests going on all over the country; some peaceful, some angry and volatile. The administration was denying any reports that a secret meeting had been held of course and as had become the norm, was spewing the nonsensical rhetoric of a raving lunatic. Press conferences were full of explanations and excuses of coups requiring military cooperation and compliance; a rationale that was both frightening and somehow comforting. Knowing that there were so many moving parts; so many variables to a government takeover and that his ego had kept him from realizing that very thing, was slightly relieving. She was sure that having someone so incredibly stupid, however manipulative, as the head of the country was a blessing in disguise as his ignorance and underestimation of the public had bought the country some time.

The day that she had never wanted to end finished as most often did, with her sleeping soundly in front of the television. He could never bring himself to wake her and the thought of sleeping without her for one night let alone for the rest of his life brought him to his knees. So like he did every night that she didn't quite make it into their bed, he gently climbed on to the couch and under the blanket careful not to wake her. He had perfected this, laying on the opposite end of the sofa and sliding his legs next to hers so at least their knees could spoon and he could keep from disturbing her, while still touching her, hearing her breathe and being there at a moment's notice. He would lie there watching her sleep; bathed in the light of the television, that puppy dog curled up at her side, wondering how he was going to do this. He could just make out the tsunami on the horizon, and this was the one time during his day that he allowed himself to feel the undertow. He could squeeze his eyes shut tight until the hot tears rolled down his cheeks and dripped into his ears. The one time in his day that no one would see how fucking terrified he was; how loosely he was keeping it all together. Finally the exhaustion would take over and he would drift into a restless sleep fraught with dreams he could never quite remember, knowing in the morning it would feel like he hadn't slept at all.

He fell asleep sometime before the timer ran out on the television and woke up with a start in the pitch black. Once he realized where he was he sat as still as stone trying to hear her breathe in the darkness. She would never know that this happened every night, and he would never tell her. He would wake, stop, listen, breathe a sigh of relief and then fix her pillow and blanket, careful not to wake her. Tonight he laid there for a long time afterwards, wishing he could wrap his arms around her and never let go; the events of today, both the sour and the sweet still on his mind. He thought back to the conversation they had had on their walk back to the house, and decided that some time away might be just what the doctor ordered. He shook his head at the thought of how shitty that once innocent figure of speech had become. Making memories he thought, as exhaustion once again won tonight's battle. They'd make new memories he thought and stifled a sob knowing that those memories would only be made for him.

9

She awoke disoriented; rubbing her eyes and looking around the living room, trying to remember how last night ended. The dog was no longer lying next to her and she could smell the coffee and hear the never ending clinking the spoon made around the sides of his mug. Smiling she wondered how dissolved he needed the sugar to be. Sometimes the first five never made it past the first two and her smile faded slightly as she realized that yesterday would not be a repeat. She felt very foggy and disconnected; her head seemed too heavy for her shoulders and it made her neck ache. Her attempts to sit up convinced her that being vertical was overrated and she decided to lie there for a while trying to piece together a dream that was floating around in her mind, just out of reach. She could only grasp images that made no sense and she knew that if she tried too hard to remember, it would disappear altogether and be the thing that possibly, finally would drive her mad. She closed her eyes and breathed a heavy sigh; frustrated and wishing for yesterday. She chuckled and shook her head. Yesterday. YESTERDAY is what you're wishing for? If we're handing out wishes, yesterday better get in fucking line. The noise brought him out of the kitchen, his head backlit and haloed in the sunlight from what was shaping up to be another once in a lifetime, beautiful fall day. He looked surprised to see her awake, thinking the giggle must have come from inside a dream, and smiled when her eyes met his. Cupping her cheek, he handed her his mug and kissed her forehead before he went back into the kitchen to fix himself his own cup. Once again she could hear the over zealous stirring and his announcement that he was going to shower. She supposed another day of playing hooky was out of the question and thought solemnly that it was best for her to spend the day in bed anyway.

By the time he had kissed her goodbye and promised her that he would check in on both of the children, she was already exhausted from the cup of coffee and her trip up the stairs. She heard the front door close as she and her faithful companion had crawled under the covers of the still made bed. She had the news on again; she just couldn't seem to help herself and she fell fast asleep as soon as her head hit the pillow.

10

It was late morning when she swam to the surface from the depths of sleep, again not quite sure at first where she was and how she had gotten there. Sleeping in the daylight had never agreed with her; she'd never been much of a napper. She had always seemed to awaken feeling somewhat lost and never knowing what time it was. This time though, as disoriented as she was, she had brought a little more of that same dream out with her. It was a little bit closer to her; a little more real. She still struggled with the details, but whatever it was had left her with both feelings of apprehension and resolve. She looked to the dog for answers, but the terrier's yawning and stretching explained nothing.

Sitting up in bed slowly, she pushed her hair off of her forehead, reached for the remote, and looked at her phone for both her messages and the time. Realizing that she was late for her meds, she opened the nightstand drawer and checked for the stash of protein bars. Of course he had made sure that they were stocked. Forcing one down slowly, her usual lack of appetite a glaring contrast to the sweet hunger she had experienced yesterday. She had no intention of spending the rest of her day stationed with her head against the toilet, so food before meds it was.

The first pill was sliding slowly down her throat when his face came on the screen and the sound of his voice like nails on a chalkboard slammed her back into that morning's dream. She was standing on a runway enveloped in fog, a plane in the distance. Not just any plane though, but his plane, the official plane, and she could hear his laugh, not from inside the aircraft, but almost from above... coming from the fog. She could see him then, standing at the top of the stairs in front of the gaping hole that was the door to the plane. He was holding a can of his seltzer. She could see the label as he lifted it into the air and toasted with the slogan, "Water is life, but have you LIVED?" And then she was back in her room. Sitting on the bed, choking on her water. Wiping her mouth, she tried desperately to hold on to that vision and pull it over her head like a blanket; climbing inside. But that was all she could remember; nothing else would come no matter how hard she grasped at it.

11

The next month or so was a blur of doctor appointments, second opinions, tests, third opinions, referrals from friends and fourth opinions. Everyone knew someone who was an expert and everything was "worth a try". One visit after another was to appease friends and family and to reassure them upon her inevitable demise that they had done all that they could. She realized even if no one else did, that whatever motions she was going through right now were all for the benefit and peace of mind of those who would still be upright when she no longer could be. As tiring as it all was, she endured it because the poking and prodding was nothing compared to the pain she could see in their eyes.

The holidays came and went. There was nothing she could do to make them normal. Nothing she could do to diffuse that dark cloud that hung over the last of everything. Had she taught them enough? Would the traditions she had so carefully cultivated survive? They had never really paid too much attention because they knew she would always be there. The regret on their faces was almost too much to bear and these times in their lives that they should most enjoy and remember were covered in the tarnish of future holidays that would be spent without her. She hoped that someday they would only remember the times when they were together before everything changed forever; before they knew what it was like to miss someone who was standing in front of them. It was ironic that the one who had been given no hope at all, spent all of her time doing the hoping.

The last doctor that she agreed to see was the cousin of a wife of a dear friend of the family. She had waited until the unpleasantness of the holidays had passed and had only consented to see this last "specialist" because this particular friend had suffered a meltdown when she had initially refused. It seemed that they had gotten down to the last of the people who knew people that could work miracles, and she was grateful that after this last act of acquiescence she would be allowed to die in peace.

This latest and last physician was a devotee and expert in alternative medicine, therapies, and treatments. It was a route they had traveled down many times in the last few months; and it was in fact the exact adamant argument that induced her friend's meltdown. So here she was, his hand in hers, walking into yet another office to await another dead end, and suffer the downward eyes and fidgety fingers of yet another medical staff that wouldn't know quite what to say. It never became normal to comfort people you didn't know and would never see again, but somehow she found herself doing it every time.

Dozens of past test results examined, blood work poured over and a physical examination later, they once again found themselves sitting across a large desk from an empty chair awaiting more of the same bad news. There was a bit of a different vibe in this room she couldn't help but notice. This office, this whole facility lacked the sterility of every one of the dozens they had visited. The walls were hued with soft shades of purples, greys and periwinkles and a very spa like smell and sound seemed to permeate every room they entered. Gone were the ultra bright lights and freezing exam room temperatures, replaced instead with warm candlelit and incense infused spaces that screamed tranquility. It was all very different, it was all very nice, but it did not instill hope. Nothing could.

The doctor was older than they had expected, a Woodstock hippie that dressed the part. She was soft- spoken and almost frighteningly calm, with silver through her hair and glasses that hung around her neck. The wrinkles etched gently into her face reminded her patient of the effect the ocean has on glass, as if time itself had deliberately planned each one. She had spoken very little during the examination; only pleasantries really, and told them very little about what she thought she could do for them. Her touch was soothing and her hands were much softer and warmer than all of the other hands that hadn't bothered to disguise their cold water washes and use of antibacterial gel.

The doctor entered the office, and closing the door behind her, crossed the room to where they were seated side by side. She stopped behind them and lightly patted their shoulders before she sat down across from them at her desk and smiling folded her hands beneath her chin. They knew that look; they'd grown accustomed to it. He squeezed her hand and she smiled the smile he had seen many times before, the one that said that something she'd heard a dozen times would not devastate her.

The doctor's conclusion was exactly as they had expected, and she was far and away more upset than the couple sitting before her. Her belief in alternative and ancient treatments had convinced her that she would be able to do what no other physician had been capable of, but she had underestimated the advancement of the disease, and it frustrated and saddened her.

Once again the couple found themselves comforting someone they had just met and over an hour was spent in her office regaling their love story as the doctor listened intently with misted eyes. She listened as they told her about the countries they would never visit and the grandbaby she would never meet, and the struggle to make every day their very best day. She reached across the desk and held the doctor's hand thanking her for her time, and grabbing her purse, stood up to leave knowing that they had overstayed their allotted appointment time. It wasn't unusual for them to get this kind of a reaction, even from uptight professionals, so when this laid back, new age, peace and love practitioner showed such emotion, it didn't really take them aback... until she completely lost it as she reached out her arms and grabbed them both tightly to say goodbye. Her shoulders heaved as tears flowed down those etched cheeks, wetting the glasses that hung around her neck. She released them and told them that she would be in touch and that she wasn't giving up. Clutching them to her one last time, she promised that she would email them a few book titles; some alternative therapies, meditation and such that might help them through the hard times. She wiped her eyes as she reached for the door handle, and opening the door, watched them walk down the hall away from her. The deep ache in the chasm of her soul told her that she had been forever changed.

12

The book titles were already in his inbox when he checked his email later that evening, and he promised her he'd go to the library on his way home from the office to see if he could find them. It was more than any of the other dozens of white coats had offered them, and even if it was only to help with the emotional and mental manifestations of this insanity, they would take it. For months now, he had been startled awake by her crying out in her sleep. In the beginning it had only been occasionally, but now it had become much more frequent and it scared him. She never spoke of nightmares, and he dare not mention it for fear that he would remind her of terrors of which she had no memory.

Yes, meditation sounded like an awesome idea.

She didn't dare tell him about the dreams. They had gotten worse; more intense, more ominous. She could never seem to crawl out of them at night and she supposed it was the meds keeping her under. In fact, she had suspected the constant medicinal cocktail extravaganza was the culprit for the nightmares in the first place. In the daytime she took bits and pieces out of her mid morning naps and hurriedly tried to scrawl them in a pad that she kept on her nightstand. It was unintelligible, nonsensical gobbledygook. The only common thread that ran through every fitful sleep was the man in the Capital. It was a presence really, a sense that he was at the center of every frightening unconscious thought. It was as if he was in the room every time she awoke. How could she even attempt to explain them to him when she could barely string them together herself? She knew her husband well enough to know that he would worry himself sick about the disease's progression, about her meds, and a million other things. She was dying, but they were both suffering, so when he came home that night with the books the doctor had recommended, all she could think of was that meditation was an awesome idea.

13

They were hoping that the meditation would also come in handy with the anxiety that came with the constant barrage of insanity coming from an administration hell bent on being the very LAST administration their country would ever have. They had done a pretty good job of sweeping the unpleasantness of their leaked meeting under the carpet, but those in the resistance knew that it only meant that they had just learned how to keep their plan out of the media. He gave a speech each and every day. Each one aimed at a different politician, discrediting their record and ruining their good name; brainwashing the population and leaving every citizen standing in an undercurrent of distrust. Every day he held a new press conference, stacking lie upon lie, boasting of his accomplishments, bragging strangely enough about the fact that he had never had a drop of alcohol, and somehow managing to make every stint in front of the camera an ad for his flavored seltzer water. His rants would turn into rambling, almost unintelligible babble that always ended with a smear campaign directed towards whomever was in his sights that day. Every day more dangerous propaganda spewed from his lips under the guise of saving the country.

The nation had just suffered through the longest government shutdown in it's history; a temper tantrum thrown by a giant toddler not getting his way. With an economy that had grown more fragile with each passing year of his reign, it took mere weeks for a shutdown to drag the nation to the brink of disaster. Hundreds of thousands of people out of work had foreclosed on their homes, whole towns that had relied on tourism suffered economic meltdowns and the domino effect had triggered a near financial collapse. The threats and the act of what could only be described as holding the country hostage were all in the name of securing a wall at the southern border. The shutdown was the political equivalent to a toddler holding their breath until their illogical childish demands were met. Presently, the current dark cloud hanging over the nation was his fabrication of a national emergency to illicit funds for his idiocracy; a smokescreen that was only meant to distract from his ultimate usurpation of power. Already there was talk of his next attack on democracy as word leaked that he would move to close all borders to not only anyone trying to enter, but to it's own citizens trying exit.

They had continued padding their mattress and the fear that the borders might actually be closed caused them to plan that much talked about trip. Knowing that court battles over his invention of an emergency could take months, and that they were still hanging their hopes on an indictment; of someone doing the right thing, they decided to make it an extended vacation. Once they had returned they were certain that they would never be able to leave again.

Almost a week after that last doctor's appointment, she was having a relatively good morning; awake and actually attempting laundry, (a chore she had spent her life dreading but now was excited to accomplish when she possessed the energy. Conversely, she always seemed to be too sick to grocery shop) when her phone rang. It was a number she did not recognize, and while it was her habit to let those go to voicemail (couldn't waste one of her precious moments on bullshit) for some reason she knew that she should answer it. It was Dr. Woodstock as they had started to lovingly refer to her between themselves, and she was asking if they would come in to see her sooner than later. Trying not to sound skeptical because the meditation was slowly coming along and starting to be of some comfort, she grudgingly agreed to talk to him about bringing her in. Dr. Woodstock assured her that she wasn't trying to convince anyone that there was a game changer up her sleeve, and that she just wanted to talk about some supplements that may offer some relief. She hung up, fully prepared NOT to mention this conversation to him. After all... MORE shit to take? Really?

The burst of morning energy had tuckered her out and she took her round of late morning meds and crawled under the covers with her furry companion. Asleep as soon as her head hit the pillow, she didn't hear him as he changed his clothes and snuggled up next to her and their old lady baby.

He hadn't been sleeping very well, and a slow day at the office had given him just the excuse he needed to catch a nap and spend even 5 more minutes with his bride. He propped himself up on one elbow, staring at her for a long time as she slept. There wasn't a curve of her face that he hadn't memorized. Not a mole, freckle or tiny scar that he hadn't named. He spent too much of his time lately trying to imagine how he would ever lie in this bed without her, and how he would survive when he looked beside him and she was no longer there. He was constantly trying to prepare himself for this empty bed and always realized that much like he could have never prepared to fall in love with her, there was no way he could ever prepare to lose her. He cuddled up next to her, the rhythm of her breath a familiar comfort that lulled him right to sleep.

The screams ripped him out of the cocoon of unconsciousness and he managed to catch the dog before she fell off the bed in an effort to get away from the shrieking. The daytime nap had disoriented him and he impulsively started to shake her and scream her name, trying desperately to silence the caterwauling. Her eyes flew open and she stared at him as if she had never seen him before, and it was obvious that in that split second she had no idea where she was. He saw the recognition creep slowly back into her eyes as her arms flew around his neck and she buried her face into his chest.

Her heart was deafening as it thudded in her ears, drowning out his voice as he tried to soothe her. She wasn't sure how long she stayed there, safe in his embrace as he rocked her; his hands tangled in her hair, shushing her softly and whispering into her ear as she sobbed. She tried to remember; tried to grasp it as it started to fade like hot breath on a cold day. What time was it? She couldn't remember falling asleep in the dark. Was it dark? She opened one eye and peered over his shoulder at the window; the daylight only causing more confusion. Why was he home? Had she lost a day? Days even? She was in their room, not in a hospital. She tried desperately to rationalize what was happening and talk herself out of the fact that she was dying NOW. RIGHT NOW.

Finally she drew away from him, pleading with her eyes for some explanation as to what was happening. He smoothed the hair from her face, kissed the tracks of her tears and pulled her back down on the bed as she snuggled into the crook of his arm. It was time to talk about the screaming; it was time to talk about the dreams.

He told her how he had listened to the nightmares and she told him what she could remember; which wasn't much. Neither one of them thought it was too far of a stretch to assume that falling asleep on the news had contributed to the terror she was experiencing, but agreed after trying to decipher the scrawl on the pad that turning off the TV would not completely rectify it. Reluctantly she told him about Dr. Woodstock's phone call earlier in the day and they decided that speaking to her about this and adding some supplements might not be the worst idea, and wiping her still damp eyes, she reached for her phone.

14

The very next morning, they found themselves back in the soothing spa like atmosphere of Dr. Woodstock's facility. This time not in her office, but in a dimly lit room that smelled of eucalyptus and lavender. Comfy orthopedic chaise lounges, almost invisible glass cocktail tables adorned with candles and a cart with self serve, fruit infused water were the only furniture in the room. They poured themselves some of the lemon water that was provided and melted into the couches to wait for the doctor to join them.

She entered the room and while motioning for them to stay comfortable, took a seat on the edge of a lounger across from them. Out of her pockets she took four pill bottles and put them in front of her on the glass table. She proceeded to explain to them that she had devoted her life to helping those that could not be helped by conventional methods; succeeding more often than not. She always approached every case as an eventual success, and had a hard time giving up no matter the prognosis. She'd been doing this for decades, but never had she sunk into the depths of despair that followed their first visit. She couldn't really explain why, certainly she'd been among the terminal more times than she dared count, but the darkness that enveloped her as she watched them walk away from her that day had left her bereft and broken. She knew that easing the suffering in the time that was left was of little consolation, but it was a gift that she had the power to give…well that, and the gift of options. She went through the supplements with them. Some were for pain management, some to calm the mind and the nerves, and some were for sleep. Glancing at each other and then the doctor, they figured it was as good a time as any to speak to her about their vacation plans and the nightmares.

She listened to their concerns about the nightmares and could see that they were both worried. There was no way to tell if the dreams were a byproduct of the meds, the disease or her mental state, but regardless, the supplements she was supplying should at least provide a little relief. It was obvious that the political climate was contributing significantly to the night terrors, and that brought the doctor to one of the most important conversations she would ever have.

In the times when she failed, when the universe bested her and souls were beyond her grasp, Dr. Woodstock offered her patients unconventional options to ease their suffering. Most of these potions were a band- aid on a bullet hole; temporary relief for a permanent condition. Only once in her lengthy career had she offered anyone a permanent solution, and although she had never expected to ever offer it to another, somewhere in the back of her mind she knew that there would come another time when mercy outweighed logic. The fact that they would be on a lengthy vacation in the midst of the current threats being lowered by the president made her very anxious, and it scared her tremendously to think that they may get stranded during a medical crisis. Still, she knew the gravity of their situation and understood their need to have this time together because there was no telling how much of it was left. Advising them against it was not an option.

She sat across from the couple after explaining each of the supplements and how to take them, and took a deep breath. They sat on their comfy chaise lounges growing uncomfortable as they watched her face grow flushed; wringing her hands like she was trying to remove her fingers. The doctor sighed heavily as she explained that what she was about to relate to them was one of the least professional things she could ever do, about one of the least professional things she had ever done.

Dr. Woodstock held on to the edge of the lounger with both hands as she told them about the love of her life. It was close to two decades ago now, and she had met him while on her own holiday. It was a whirlwind romance that had taken her by surprise having spent most of her life as a solo act. He was her polar opposite, the passion to her stoic, the crazy to her calm, the ying to her yang. They were together only a few months when he got his diagnosis. It was devastating.

Walking to the table, she poured herself a glass of water and chuckled, seeming to forget that they were in the room as she whispered about having loved and lost. She turned and taking a long drink rubbed her eyes and smiled, waving away the pity she saw in their eyes as she described their last few months together. They too had taken a long trip when all of their options had been exhausted; his dream trip to the rain forest. They had both been prepared that he might not return home. It was a magical trip, despite her overwhelming feelings of helplessness. She had spent her life caring and curing, and the one she most needed to save was beyond her reach.

She watched him slip a little further away day after day, more and more of their time away being spent trying to recover from the simplest of tasks.

One afternoon she learned about a healing ceremony taking place in a nearby village from one of the hotel employees, and by nightfall they were sitting around a fire with the locals. After devoting her life to alternative medicine she was eager to try anything that could help him, and while the advancement of the disease was beyond a cure, she would try anything that brought even the tiniest bit of relief.

They couldn't understand one word said during the ceremony, but when every chant was over, and every prayer had been said, the priest came to them and took him by the shoulders. Standing toe to toe, he pressed his cocoa colored forehead against her love's furrowed brow and closed his eyes; a guttural groan emerging from his throat. It was as if the two were in a trance, and for an instant she though that this witch doctor was curing him right before her eyes. She rolled her eyes and shook her head smirking the way one does when remembering a feeling of stupidity; her hands covering her eyes trying to block out the memory. The couple's eyes were transfixed on her, realizing that she was back in the rain forest in front of that fire with her love. She never met their gaze as she told them how a young man approached and led her into a hut, grabbed her hand, and into it placed two round, smooth pellets. They resembled chocolate covered coffee beans; larger than pearls but smaller than gumballs and as hard as pebbles. He told her that the priest knew her partner did not have much time and this was a choice, a peaceful alternative… this was mercy. An ancient herb known only to this tribe, handed down by generations of priests, and given only to those that still had the ability to make their own choice. It was mercy dispensed to end the suffering, by the suffering.

The doctor had crossed the room and was once again seated back on the edge of the chaise staring down at her cupped hands as though she was seeing the priest's gift right there in her palm. She finally met their gaze with tear filled eyes and told them that when the end came, they had spent his last day in the jungle, next to a waterfall, holding each other and not saying a word. That night they dissolved the pellet in his very last beer. It didn't taste like anything, it didn't smell like anything and it took it's time. He became tired, then drowsy and finally just fell asleep like any other night. Twelve hours later he was gone and she was alone; the most alone she had ever been in her life. She never questioned his decision or her role in carrying it out, although there were many times that she thought about the twelve hours it would take to join him. She could have kept this alternative to herself, not told him, selfishly let him suffer so she could bathe in the glow of his life just a little while longer. He deserved peace and dignity and the right to make that decision, and she so wanted that peace for him.

She wiped the tears from her cheeks and breathed deeply as she pulled a tissue from her pocket. The doctor could feel the pity radiating almost in waves off of the couple; their wide, tear filled eyes still upon her. She smiled and assured them she was fine but that there was a very definite basis for regaling such a personal and painful tale.

She had kept that second pellet for years, at first always certain that she would be the one to benefit from it's relief. In the immediate days and months after his death she would look at it daily, talk herself out of it and promise that tomorrow would be the day. The months turned into years; the pain she once wore like a second skin covering every inch of her had slowly become more like a toothache. What remained of the priest's gift was tucked safely away, out of sight but never out of mind. She had never told anyone about this miracle, but as time went on she realized that it might be a gift that under the most dire of circumstances could be shared. So last year she returned to the small village looking for peace; some for herself and some to bring home with her.

Standing up, she pulled a miniature key from a pocket inside her coat and crossed the room to her desk. She unlocked a small drawer, and from it produced a blue-green bottle that looked like it was made of sea glass. Holding the bottle in one hand, she relocked the drawer, slipped the key back into her coat pocket and once again returned to her seat on the edge of the chaise lounge facing the couple.

All at once he knew where this was going; where this conversation was headed and his mind started to reel. He watched his wife as her eyes followed the doctor's trip back to her seat and saw her mouth hang open ever so slightly as the realization came to her too. Was he sweating? Was he freezing? Yes to both. Involuntarily his hand reached for her and found a clammy hand reaching back. A million questions all at once racing through his head and unsure if he would hear what the doctor was going to say next above the din of his own screaming thoughts. She squeezed his hand, her sigh catching in her throat as she tried to stay focused. She told the doctor to go on… his brave wife wanted to hear the rest and he closed his eyes and took a deep breath.

Back at home, they sat on the couch, the little bottle on the coffee table before them. They hadn't spoken much since leaving the doctor's office and now as they sat mesmerized by the iridescent glass and it's contents, the silence seemed deafening. It was a ridiculous suggestion, an idea rooted in both mercy and compassion, but nonetheless not a notion that either one of them was willing to take seriously. Yet there they sat, staring at that ridiculous suggestion, neither wanting to believe that it would ever come to that. A week later, those "chocolate covered coffee beans" packed among the socks, underwear and extra hats and gloves, slipped unnoticed out of the country; their charges having convinced themselves of their triviality, and sure that all four of them would return home together.

15

The election year trudged along, each party having chosen their candidates and the last months of his reign dwindling down to an end. He had ramped up the rhetoric, using every free moment in front of the camera to nurture the seeds he had planted in his follower's minds about the upcoming change in administration. He hinted at requiring a military presence to keep the peace and his remarks smacked of a revolution even as both parties constantly accused him of threatening to undermine democracy. Attempts to remove him from office amidst rumors of a coup had been unsuccessful and now the country was in a holding pattern; just trying to get to the election of a new leader and the business of trying to heal a nation and repair the fundamentals it was built upon.

They were a little more than a month or so into their trip; lifting a beer to their lips in a quaint pub when he saw the headline roll across the TV over the bar. She turned to follow his gaze and set her pint back on the table unable to blink as she stared at the television. The Vice President was dead. As far as they could tell it was a freak accident. He had slipped in the shower, hit his head and never regained consciousness. They struggled to figure out what this meant for the state of the country and for a split second they even thought about going home. After speaking to the kids, cooler heads prevailed and they knew that sitting tight and not panicking was their best bet. They had been diligently watching the signs of border closure, and as easy as it would have been to tune out, stay away from the news and lose themselves in this adventure, they had paid very close attention to news and were never too far from a TV. It wasn't very difficult as they were still slaves to the disease and many days were spent never leaving whatever hotel room or bed and breakfast they were guests of.

They ordered food and another pint and sat eating and watching the BREAKING NEWS unfold thousands of miles away, until it was obvious that there were no new facts, just the same story being regurgitated a hundred different ways. They were traveling tomorrow, and they knew that the supreme leader would be moving his next chess piece by the time they arrived at their destination. The Madam secretary, once without so much of a chance of taking his place, was now one step behind him, ready to lead the country should the cracks in his facade cause his castle to crumble. He would be on the attack, saying anything that he thought would undermine her credibility and strike fear in the hearts of his sheep, even before his running mate's body was cold.

The check was paid and they walked arm and arm back to their hotel, deciding that there would be no television on at all for the rest of the night. There wasn't any doubt that Dr. Woodstock's sleep supplements and magic elixirs would come in handy after the latest machine gun round of events. Meds taken and water swallowed, they curled up next to each other in the dark; the lights from the street peering through the curtains; keeping watch over their packed suitcases. They had slept side by side every night on this trip, an unexpected benefit that came from one room encompassing their entire living quarters. The nightmares had subsided quite a bit, he could only assume thanks to the doctor's potions and pills.

There were many bad days since leaving home, and they had tried to see as much of six countries in 5 weeks as they could. Some days she was racked with so much pain and such profound weakness that every cell in his body ached with hers in unison. They soon realized that almost every hotel was in possession of a wheelchair, and even on days when the first five had been downright adamant about staying in bed, they would get her out to see just one thing that she would never see again. He curled up closer, pulled her a little tighter to him, and buried his head in her hair, finally succumbing to sleep with thoughts of a more restful continuation of their holiday that would begin the next time he opened his eyes.

16

She lay there watching the waves and imagining how much easier it would be to survive her worst of days with the help of salt water and sand. Their travel day had been overwhelming and now as the breeze wafted over her skin, softly rippling the corner of her towel, it seemed like a lifetime ago. They had set up camp on the beach in a purposefully strategic spot; not too far from the resort or surf side bar, but far enough from foot traffic to relax and suffer in peace if need be. From her comfy vantage point on her oversized beach bed she could see just about everything and already realized that she could watch all the comings and goings at the bar, her large sunglasses and floppy hat cloaking her spying eyes. She had forgotten how long it had been since she had been able to sit quietly, unbothered and people watch, and how much she had missed it. Such a simple pleasure really; and like so many others, one she had taken for granted.

He had been told…no, ORDERED to go into the water and enjoy himself, another attempt to convince him that this trip couldn't only be about watching her die. She had promised that she would dip her toes in later after she had rested and hopefully regained a little strength back. He begrudgingly walked to the shoreline, turning around every so often to see her waving and blowing kisses. Her toes curled and her eyes closed as she stretched the stretch of contentment. It was the kind of contentment that can only exist with the purest appreciation of every single second; the kind that comes when you know that no matter what you do, you have nothing left to lose.

Every day was spent in the same perfect spot he had reserved for the duration of their stay. Even the worst of the worst days could be spent on the beach bed watching the vacationers come and go and the palm trees wave. She became very familiar with the bar's regular visitors; those whose holiday was more of a residence than a brief respite from the world outside. There was Frank, who had 60 years of tan, an amazing head of grey hair, an endless amount of cash and a 24 year old girlfriend named Destini who made sure she introduced herself as Destini with an "I". They had met while Frank was undergoing cardiac rehab and Destini was visiting her grandmother. Roberta and Stan looked to be in their late seventies and spent their afternoons at the Surfside after mornings of golf or tennis. They were both retired, had three children; two boys and a girl, and eight grandchildren. Renee and Isabel were sisters in their thirties, that had just sold their successful cupcake bakery as a franchise and were celebrating with an extended fall off the grid. Last but not least was Joel, a retired plastic surgeon and his much younger wife Sylvia. Sylvia was never NOT wearing gold, and Joel was never NOT wearing his toupee. Smiling through it all behind the bar was Marty, which she was sure was not his given name. He knew how to keep them all happy, drinking and coming back for more.

They were a very entertaining group that interestingly enough hardly ever interacted with each other. A word here and there; they very obviously all recognized each other from the bar, but it struck her that this was the perfect example of people wrapped up in their own lives and just not paying attention to what was going on around them. She watched them arrive and listened as they regaled the events from the night before, or stewed about their golf game. It was always disappointing when she slept through one of Destini's tantrums or missed one of Sylvia's tits popping out of her way too small bikini only to hear her feign surprise and embarrassment. Her stifled laughter always caused him to look up from his book, and smile at her the way you would an impetuous child, and raising her hand to his lips would go back to reading without a word.

Her nights had become more restless. The nightmares were finding their way through the supplements like headlights slicing through a thick fog. He had been trying desperately to keep her away from the news but the dreams were back and it didn't seem to matter whether she had seen the television or not. Questions were swirling around the Vice President's unexpected death and the supreme leader's questionable and suspicious actions leading up to the accident. Congress had also subpoenaed his tax returns when he failed to produce them by the required deadline and vowing to stop working with the opposition party until their investigations of him had ceased, he had gone underground; disappeared to avoid the fallout. The madam secretary was working feverishly to get the votes needed to remove him from office and force the administration to divulge his whereabouts. It was a mess that was heading towards endgame and he was determined to keep her away from as much of it as he could, and yet still she woke up screaming.

Her residency on the beach bed was entering it's second week when a new visitor visited the surfside bar. A tall, broad shouldered guy who looked to be in his thirties; he was dressed like the beach shop had thrown up all over him. A big floppy hat that clashed with his electric blue dayglo Hawaiian shirt, he definitely did not blend in. She had never seen him before and figured he was just starting his holiday so maybe in his excitement he had been a little heavy handed with the resort wear. She saw Marty turn around and reach into the fridge behind him, pull out a can, open it and set it on the bar. The label was immediately recognizable and made her heart skip a beat as she flashed back to her dream on the runway. She couldn't read the flavor from her spot beneath the palm tree, but the large orange letters that read LIVED seltzer water were unmistakable. He thanked Marty and left with the seltzer, his flip flops spraying sand as he walked away.

She fell asleep in the shade and was jolted awake by the high shrill of laughter coming from the bar. It was Destini flying solo while Frank took his afternoon nap and she was shamelessly flirting with Marty who looked over at her in the shade of her palm tree and shook his head. He was a sweet guy who had many times come over to check on her while her husband was walking on the beach or taking a swim. She was sure he'd asked Marty for an extra pair of eyes when he wasn't in the immediate vicinity and they'd had a handful of really nice conversations in his absence. A few times she had even been strong enough to sit at the bar with her husband while he was cutting fruit and stocking the bar for the busy afternoons. Right now that nice guy was fending off the advances of the girlfriend of one of his best tippers and he needed saving. While she tried to muster the strength to get off the lounger, his savior arrived wearing a floppy hat and an electric blue shirt covered with bright yellow macaws. Destini's attention having been immediately diverted, Marty let out a deep sigh. "Mister resort wear" ignored her like a pro and grabbing his can of LIVED orange flavored seltzer, left her sucking on her straw and rolling her eyes.

17

For only the second time since arriving in paradise, the first five gave her the thumbs up. She knew that her bad days were now starting to outnumber the good, so whenever she got a good one she made it the best day of her life. She rolled over and snuggled against him, burying her face in the nape of his neck and pressing her breasts into his back. She felt the squeeze of his hand as he rolled toward her and smiled when he saw the sparkle in her eyes. They made love to the sound of the waves crashing outside their room and then ate breakfast on the veranda watching the early morning joggers leave divots in the wet sand. Such days were fleeting and they both knew that in mere hours she would be weak and sleeping and one day closer to the inevitable, so down to the ocean they went.

Her favorite beach pastime by far was seashell hunting. Some of her most cherished memories as a child were spending hours on the beach, sun kissed and toe headed, searching for just the right shell. The feeling of knowing the right one when she saw it, and the elation as her skinny legs carried her running back to her mother's small beach chair was one of her most cherished memories. It was something that she hadn't been able to do since she arrived and today she was going to get some beauties to bring home as a reminder of their last time away together. They walked along the shoreline, her eyes cast downward in search of the perfect specimens to fill her suitcase with. He wondered out loud what kind of renovations they were doing to this section of the hotel. She looked up to see that they were approaching the end of the resort's property and massive tarp like curtains had been erected around the balconies and verandas that jutted out from the end of the hotel. They strolled a little further before turning around and heading back down the beach towards their spot beneath the palm tree, once again passing the construction zone at the far end of the resort. Squinting through her sunglasses, she raised her hand instinctively to her forehead to shield her eyes from the glare of the sun. The tarps reminded her of a shower curtain draped around a curved rod, and seemed a little flimsy to be any sort of protection from construction debris. At first she couldn't quite put her finger on what seemed odd, until she realized that there was no scaffolding or building materials near the renovation site; no workers in the vicinity even though it was late morning. She shrugged her shoulders, thinking that she really didn't give a shit about the rights and wrongs of construction being done on a building she might never see again on this trip let alone in this lifetime, when she caught movement out of the corner of her eye.

It took her a second to focus, and her immediate thought was to wonder if he had bought more than one outfit. She straightened up and cocked her head to the side as she watched the floppy hat and electric blue shirt enter a door nearest the tarps. She glanced over at her love to see him lost in the work of finding her the perfect shell, and looking back towards the hotel, saw that "mister resort wear" had disappeared inside. Wrong door? Part of the hotel staff? Neither idea seemed plausible. Again, she shrugged her shoulders and throwing her arms around her husband's neck, kissed him hard as her hat flew into the sea.

Late morning meant a round of meds and a little nap if she wanted to continue on with the rest of a perfect day. He lay down next to her on their reserved little corner of heaven and raised the canopy to shield them from the imminent noontime sun. She fell asleep almost immediately; her cheek nestled into the spot on his chest it had carved out over the last quarter century. He listened to her breathing and running his hand down her arm, smiled at what joy one simple breath could bring him. His hand cupped hers and he realized that she was still holding a shell that she had found on their walk. It was broken and imperfect. Its edges were softened and rounded from years of the sea beating it into submission, yet its core was strong and intact. Just like his beautiful bride. It wasn't long before her breath and the breeze acted like the perfect sedative and he fell asleep; his cheek resting on the top of her head.

Her eyes fluttered open and her first thought was that she had dreamt NOTHING. She wasn't nervous or anxious; just rested. Her movements roused him from his nap and he woke to see her sitting up, smiling at him. She felt good and didn't want to waste a second, so she left him to finish waking up and made her way to the bar to get one of Marty's tropical concoctions. She could see "mister resort wear" turning to leave the bar, seltzer in hand as she approached, thinking he most definitely had no game when it came to dressing, but at least he was wearing a different shirt. She absentmindedly bit her bottom lip as she wondered if he really was who she saw entering the construction zone on the other side of the resort and how could one person drink THAT much fucking seltzer? When she turned back to the bar, Marty was staring at her. He told her that he had no idea who the guy was, as he opened the small fridge to reveal it completely stocked with orange flavored LIVED seltzer and made a sweeping gesture with his hand. He had paid Marty an enormous tip to keep it fully stocked 24-7 and even though the bartender thought it was weird, what the guy had given him already, and promised to give him more of, was more than he made in an entire month bartending.

She ordered the two drinks and he rolled his eyes as he realized he was out of pineapple juice. She offered to watch the bar for him. After all he'd only be gone a second and an all-inclusive resort meant no money would change hands. She promised she wouldn't steal any of his tips with a wink and he darted out from behind the bar and back towards the hotel. She stood behind the bar and took a look around, thinking she hadn't been on this side of things in close to twenty years when she had been a waitress and took over while the bartenders stocked their supplies. She'd even learned to make a few of these tropical drinks back in the day. He was back in less than five minutes carrying fruits and juices and so grateful to her, that he threw an extra shot into their drinks. Walking back to her palm tree, she yelled over her shoulder that she'd help him out anytime provided she was strong enough to stand up.

They sipped their drinks sitting in the pool, and watching the pterodactyl shaped birds do their kamikaze imitations just beyond the shoreline. She felt another shell hunt coming on, knowing that feeling this good was like Cinderella at the ball. Making her way to the pool steps, she saw him again; Hawaiian shirt billowing behind him and floppy hat bouncing as he walked. She closed one eye against the sun and cocked her head to the side as she watched him weave in and out of the lounge chairs, making his way back to the surfside bar. He must've passed three or four places to get seltzer in his travels, so why have the bar furthest away stock your favorite beverage? Maybe he was trying to get away from the wife or kids, or mother in law and the long walk was his only time to himself? People are so fucking weird she thought as their feet hit the sand.

18

She spent the next week or so horizontal, watching the regulars come and go at the bar between naps and watching "mister resort wear" become a regular, albeit quick visitor. She noticed that she could almost set her watch by him. Every day right about the time that Marty started stocking for his late afternoon, pre dinner rush, there he was, making his way through the lounge chairs. Sometimes she woke up from her nap as he was coming and sometimes she was watching his back as he walked away. Eventually, she started looking at her phone for the time and realized that he may look like he got dressed in the dark, but he was quite punctual.

Her partner in crime had been instructed to go on regular walks and he would report back to her all that had been seen and heard so that she felt like she had been walking beside him. He again pondered out loud about what was happening on the other side of the resort as more often his walks took him past the gargantuan sheets hiding an entire section of the hotel. He had noticed as she had the week before that there were no workers, no materials, nothing that even suggested renovations were being done. On his last trip along the shore that bordered that portion of the resort, he had quite by accident looked up and noticed movement on the roof. The sun in his eyes made it hard to tell if there was work being done, but he seemed to think it was a roof top deck that was being used somehow. That didn't make much sense considering it was sitting above a dozen rooms that were off limits to guests. He kissed her forehead and promising to return quickly, went back to their room to get some more sunblock. She watched as he disappeared into the courtyard, and even though it took more strength than she thought she possessed, waved Marty over to her beach bed.

Whispering, and then wondering out loud why she was whispering, she asked him what renovations they were doing on the south side of the hotel. Leaning over, he did whisper as his eyes kept sight of his bar and scanned the vicinity for rogue eavesdroppers. The official word from the resort higher ups was that there was a mold issue that needed to be remediated, but the staff's talk amongst themselves called bullshit. The entire wing of the hotel had been sealed off almost at a moment's notice; signs put up overnight. A couple of days later the buzz among the workforce was that there was an awful lot of activity in rooms that were completely sealed off. However, no one had ever actually seen any signs of anything that resembled work being done. Most of the staff held the theory that it was someONE and not someTHING that shut down that wing of the resort.

He reminded her that his country's corrupt government was overthrown almost a decade ago, and many members of the past administration were still being brought up on charges and tried for crimes against their countrymen. Fear still ran rampant because pockets of the old government's supporters still existed. It was very hard for those prosecuting the criminals to find anyone who would testify against the defendants and when they did, they went to great lengths to protect their identity and ensure their safety. There was a lot of whispering, much like he was whispering now, about what was happening on the south side. He put a hand on her shoulder, his dark skin in complete contrast to her pale complexion and pointed to the bar to show her that he had a customer. Her eyes followed him as he jogged back to his post, wondering about his theory as she watched him pouring ingredients into the blender. Would the resort put hundreds, possibly thousands of people's lives in danger to protect a witness? She didn't know.

Giving up social media was a choice she had made shortly after losing consciousness in that very first doctor's office. No good could come of the constant barrage of people she barely knew, the private messages filled with pity, and the perfect lives of others that only served to remind her of how little time she'd been given. The last time she'd ever used a search engine was when she Googled how she was going to die and even just the memory of it made the palms of her hands clammy as she reached for her phone. She took a deep breath that caught in her throat as she exhaled and typed in "LIVED SELTZER". Dozens upon dozens of images and ads for the water filled the screen and reflected in her sunglasses. She scrolled through them, unsure of what she was looking for and typed in the word "ORANGE". Her jaw dropped to her chest as her phone was flooded with countless pictures of the president holding cans of ORANGE LIVED

SELTZER WATER. Why had she never noticed this before? Holding a can as he got out of his limo, holding a can walking into the capital, holding a can as he met with foreign dignitaries. There were cans placed on podiums, in cup holders in his golf cart, and on the huge oak desk in his office. Orange, orange, orange; the flavor never changed.

She swiped through photo after photo, shaking her head in disbelief until one image made her clamp her hand over her mouth to stifle a gasp. There he stood, in the doorway of the plane, his arm raised in a toast, silver and orange can in hand. Staring so hard at the image that it almost felt like she was inside that photo, she noticed details that her nightmares had excluded. His ill fitted suit hung off him and his pant legs flowed over his shoes and onto the stair's landing like navy blue lava. His version of a smile was a sneer; his lips grotesquely pulling away from large Chiclet sized, over whitened teeth as his empty hand pointed in a wave that more closely resembled a bizarre salute. For the first time she noticed how the color of the words on the can almost perfectly matched his unnatural cheddar cheese colored spray tan, but it was the figure standing behind him that caused the blood to drain from her face. The only thing missing was the floppy hat and bright macaw covered shirt, and right in the middle of a humid tropical paradise, she began to shiver. Taking off her sunglasses and closing her eyes could not remove the image that was seared into her corneas like she had been staring at the sun too long.

His return from their room was accompanied by whistling and she quickly tossed her phone back into her bag before he reached the beach bed. She tried desperately to look normal but his whistling abruptly ended and his face immediately grew dark as he saw her forehead glistening in sweat. The artificial smile was ignored as he sat on the edge of the lounger and took her hand as he pushed his sunglasses to the top of his head. Holding his hand to her forehead, and blotting the perspiration with his towel, he was finally convinced that she did not have a fever. She managed to persuade him that she had just had a wave of nausea and needed to close her eyes for a bit, when the VERY last thing she wanted to do was close her eyes. Curling up, a hat over her face feigning sleep, it was a long time before she heard him tiptoe away and ask Marty to guard over her while he ran to the bathroom and she wondered how much time she had to cry.

19

She struggled with whether or not she should tell him that the enemy of the people and his entourage were holed up mere yards away. The world was wondering where he was, their nation was falling apart, and he was drinking seltzer with an ocean view. Why heap more worry onto the mountain that they were already suffering? They'd be gone in a week or so anyway and she wanted to save him from further stress. She assumed that "mister resort wear" was secret service of some kind and figured that the reasons he chose to trek such a distance to fetch his boss his favorite drink were two fold. Making his rounds casing the resort and it's guests was probably the main objective, throwing off anyone who might be suspicious by wandering to the furthest bar was the second. She for the life of her could not figure out why the seltzer was being stocked outside of the south wing. The only thing that made sense was that nothing that this crazy person did made any sense. He was fucking nuts. She was seeing further proof of what she already knew first hand.

Trying to keep up on the news was hard and had to be done behind his back. The nightmares were coming two and three in a night and he was adamant about keeping any and all updates about the current state of the country as far from her as possible. The TV in the room would be turned on and muted while he took a shower, she would sneak looks at her phone while he napped or went for a swim. She didn't know why she was so sure that knowing what was happening was crucial, but something was gnawing at her from the inside out. There was fresh hell coming; she could FEEL it.

That feeling came to fruition 48 hours after she'd realized that they were sleeping under the same roof as the cause of her nightmares. The press conference was held with no hint of where it was being televised from, and everything about it, every word spoken screamed COUP. He finally made the announcement that the country's borders would be closed for the "protection" of it's citizens amid bogus claims that the majority of the nation had called overwhelmingly for him to remain in office indefinitely. His takeover would become effective at the borders' closing in a month's time and would have the full backing of the nation's military. Her very first thought was that she was going to leave this world as her family and friends started to fight for their lives. Her son and husband might die defending their freedom, and her grandbaby would be born in the midst of war.

He emerged from the bathroom wet from a shower, rubbing his head with a towel to see her perched on the edge of the bed, her blanched face framed against the backdrop of a beautiful tropical twilight behind her. He could not believe that she was watching the news, and crossed the room to turn it off when he realized what was happening. He stared at it right along with her, realizing immediately that this was the beginning of the final act. Everything they had feared, everything they had dreaded was becoming reality before their eyes. They should have been standing on their balcony watching what would be one of their last sunsets in paradise. What would be one of her last sunsets EVER. Instead they were once again staring at this monster and listening to his lunacy, and something in him just snapped. He grabbed the remote and turning off the TV, gently guided her off the bed and onto the balcony. This pox on humanity wasn't going to take one more minute, not one more second from them and he told her so. They would discuss what to do next tomorrow, because right now in this moment he was going to hold his wife and look out over the ends of the earth. They stood silently facing the water as the sun went down. He was standing behind her, his arms wrapped around her waist noticing how much smaller it had become in the last few months. He could feel her body leaning against him and he knew that he would be calling room service to eat in bed next to her as she slept. The sun disappeared quickly into the water, changing the sky from a fiery orange blaze to a dusty muted blend of periwinkle and violets, and when the show was over, he carried her into the room and sat her on the bed to take all of her nighttime pills. It wasn't long before she was breathing deeply, her face sunk into the oversized hotel pillow. He stared at her as he lifted the phone off its cradle to call for food, and wondered how long he had before the screaming started.

20

She was running through the fog, feeling the runway pounding beneath her feet, knowing that it was gaining on her. She could hear the engine at first whining, and then getting closer as it became a deafening roar. She ran, wanting to look back but knowing that every glance over her shoulder would slow her down. Her feet felt like they were burning as they hit the hot pavement and she was breathing so hard that her chest hurt. She saw the runway lights breaking through the fog as the tarmac fell away and sand squished between her toes as she ran. She bolted out of the fog to find herself standing breathlessly in front of the billowing tarps that were writhing and twisting in the wind. Every cell in her body was sure that behind that looming building there was nothing but flames lapping at the earth from the bowels of hell. In slow motion she lifted her head as her gaze fell upon the roof of the hotel silhouetted against a sky that was bruised purplish red and swollen with dark storm clouds. It was then that she saw him, his face painted in a sinister grin filled with gruesome delight. It was as if he was melting, and she stood gaping as streams of orange flowed down the side of the building hitting the sand like the wax of a melted crayon. On either side of him, kneeling at his feet were statues, their heads bowed in supplication; sentries turned to stone to display their shame and forever preserve their guilt and punishment. His lips, cracked and bleeding red, became a cavernous wound as he threw his head back and convulsed with a deep, bellowing laughter that shook and cracked the sentries, freeing them from their confinement.

She steadied herself, digging into the sand as the ground trembled beneath her feet and chunks of stone landed all around her. It had started to rain. Squinting through the drops that pelted her face, she saw the sentries raise their heads as their concrete prisons fell away around them. Rain blurred her vision and she wiped her eyes trying to focus on the faces kneeling before him. Her knees started to buckle then as their eyes once downcast in humiliation, now so familiar rose to meet hers; eyes full of fear and shame, pleading silently for her forgiveness.

On the verge of giving up, defeat enveloping her soul, she stared into the eyes of her husband and son. She could feel their suffering breaking her into pieces that fell away like shattered glass. And then she heard the cry. At first almost inaudible, the sound carried away on the wind; then stronger, fighting to be heard. She had never heard this cry before, but immediately her heart recognized it as belonging to her. The infant he held in his outstretched hand flailed its arms and screamed as his laughter became demonic. Any sense of defeat was replaced by sheer fury as she steeled herself against the wind, threw her head back and screamed.

She was transported then, back to her childhood bedroom. Cross legged she sat, the fall leaves emblazoned outside her window reading the Halloween book that someday she would read to her own children year after year. The Pumpkin Giant with the Jack o' Lantern head that terrorized a mythical land by eating fat little girls and boys. A farmer, and a throw that landed a potato with perfect precision down the monster's throat, his giant orange head shattering into a million pieces as he hit the ground, freeing the people and saving every child in the kingdom.

She was still screaming as she tore her eyes away from her wailing grandchild, and looking around at the rising tide saw it glistening within the lightning strikes; the perfect shell. With one swift move she snatched it off the sand and hurled it through the air with the strength and agility of an all-star pitcher; her weak and diseased body nowhere in sight. His hands flew to the throat that was still melting and running and as he crashed to earth and the tiny human fell from his grip....

His arms were around her and even as she came out of it she couldn't stop the screaming. Her nightclothes were drenched in her own sweat. Her hair wet and pasted to her forehead like she had been in the rain, making it harder to distinguish reality from the terror on the beach. She finally heard his voice, opened her eyes, and looking into his, slumped in his arms crying a cry that he had never heard before. Through the diagnosis, and the pain, through the nightmares, he had never heard the primitive, raw, guttural howl he was hearing now coming from the depths of her soul.

The tears subsided into deep breathing from the comfort that only the purest of love could provide. As he had done countless nights before, he held, almost swaddled her in his arms, whispering in her ear and rocking her until the dream dissipated like lifting fog, and reality emerged like the sunrise they sat watching from the lounge chairs on their balcony. Finite sunrises, finite sunsets, infinite memories…..

21

Their last full day in paradise, once imagined as full of romance and remembrance, now needed to be started with a discussion about what nightmares, real and imagined waited for them when they stepped off the plane. Lack of sleep prevented the first five from giving her today's verdict, but she was powering through this shit; today was going to be amazing so help her gods. He went down to the lobby to finalize their departure the next day, promising to be back soon. She was finishing her coffee and told him she'd be wearing her bathing suit and ready for a walk on the beach and a long talk about what came next when he returned.

As soon as he disappeared into the hallway, she went into the closet and grabbed the handle of her suitcase. She remembered the day they had arrived, and the ease with which she had been able to roll her then full suitcase from the living room to the bedroom of their suite. She faced almost empty luggage now and struggled to wheel it over towards the bed. Knowing there was no way to lift it, she flipped it over onto the floor and opened it carefully, not quite sure that she remembered after more than a month which side was up and how much was left inside. On her knees she struggled to open the lock, having no idea how soon he'd be back. The third time's the charm she thought, as the lock popped up and she opened the suitcase wide on the floor. Hats and gloves, boots and heavy socks were all that were left in this case. She sat for a moment trying to remember which sock she had hid it in. Maybe the ones her brother had gotten her the day they said goodbye. Her head hung for a moment remembering the look on his face. He was a crier her brother; at the very drop of a hat. Wearing his heart on his sleeve was what she loved most about him. The other half of her brain.... they were the same person for so long. She shook her head. No time for this, she was not dead yet. She would hug him and laugh with him again.

She grabbed the socks and felt the solid cylinder that she had hidden within. How long had he been gone? She panicked a little and tossed the socks onto the bed as she slammed the suitcase shut and fumbled with the key. Sliding it into the closet and turning it upright she realized that sweating when he came back would be bad, just as she realized that the socks out of the suitcase would be equally as bad. Looking at the clock and wondering how much time had passed, she crawled from the closet and pulled the socks off the bed, trying to not exert so much energy. She sat with her back against the bed, her knees bent to her chest and reaching into the socks retrieving the blue green bottle she hadn't seen since she packed her suitcase.

It was still just as mesmerizing as the very first time she had seen it and she pressed the bottle against her forehead and heaved a heavy sigh. She couldn't let another moment pass and pulling herself up onto the bed, sat looking around the room for her beach bag. She spied it across the room, thinking that it couldn't have been further away if had been in another country, and taking a deep breath willed herself off the bed. Stumbling into the living room of their massive suite, she made it to the beach bag just in time to hear the swipe of the key card letting him in. She shoved the bottle into her bag with one hand as she thrust the socks under the armoire with the other, and pulling herself up onto the nearest chair, pasted a smile across her face as he entered the room.

He stared down at her, his head cocked to one side, and placing the key card on the armoire, cupped her cheek in his hand. She was flushed, but smiling and grabbing her hands in his, he eased her off the chair and pulled her close, pressing his cheek against hers. He was eager to get to the beach, but not eager to have any part of this day interrupted by the conversation that was to come. Tomorrow they would be stepping off a plane into a whole new world, and it was important to have a plan for their children and her declining health. The interruption was inevitable, but he was determined to make it brief. He had a surprise planned for their last night and he wanted her to be able to both stay rested and enjoy their last day.

Their seashell hunt did not take them anywhere near the south side of the resort, she couldn't bear to even catch a glimpse of it. They wandered, sometimes hand in hand, scanning the shoreline for free souvenirs. Her heart was in it, but her mind was on the one item in her beach bag that would not be coming home with her. It didn't take long before the exhaustion had set in and she knew that she was due for meds and a short nap. He wrapped his arm around her waist and playfully kicked sand over her toes as she rested her head on his "just the right height for her head" shoulder. Back at the beach bed she was sure to get her meds out of the bag herself and settled in under the cabana. He thought that he would take advantage of her nap to go back to the room and start packing their bags, but insisted on staying by her side until she fell asleep.

She lay there a long time staring at that bag, thinking about all the firsts. Their first kiss, their first fight, the first time they had sex. But the firsts were so long ago, it was the seconds and thirds and fourths and twentieths that their marriage... that their LIFE had been built upon. Their third family vacation, when the baby was so sick. The tenth time that his mom was in the hospital, and keeping him upright during the funeral and weeks that followed. The thirtieth time he brought her flowers, and the sixth time the basement flooded. Thirteen hundred Sunday dinners, followed by just as many Monday mornings. Their fourteenth year together that included fifty fights and ten threats to end it. That fifteenth anniversary trip when they danced in the street to a jazz band, and their sixteenth anniversary when they danced in their living room to the TV. Forty school concerts, twenty- two children's birthday parties, eight broken bones, twenty-five hand carved jack o' lanterns that went hand in hand with twenty –four hand made costumes. Surviving the dog's fourth birthday when she almost choked to death on a cookie. Surviving the boys fourth birthday when he almost choked on a hot dog. Hundreds of rock concerts, two enemas, too many operations, a few accidents, dozens of tear filled goodbyes at airports, thousands of tears and millions of I love you's. Like snapshots flashing before her eyes, the memories of this life kept sleep at bay. The realization of what she owed the Universe for this life kept her lying to her husband as she closed her eyes and waited for him to leave, safe in his knowledge that he would be back before she awoke.

Swinging her feet on to the sand, she sat on the edge of the bed and took a deep breath as she reached into her bag. With both hands still inside to hide the bottle she popped open the metal latch and let the smooth round pellet roll into her hand. In one smooth move, she slipped her hand into the pocket of her cover up and into a plastic baggie she had been carrying with her to protect her phone. She dug in the sand with her toes watching Marty and the regulars at the surf side bar. She thought she would go to the spa and get her very last pedicure, she thought she might never see her children again. She looked out over the ocean, felt the breeze blowing on her face; watched the sun shimmer on the water. She looked at the horizon and smiled knowing that endings were also beginnings. She thought about fear that had turned into resolution. She thought about one last gift. She thought... no she knew that eventually they would forgive her and one day they would understand.

Looking at her phone, already regretting not having napped and seeing the time chuckled and thought of the old adage "I'll sleep when I'm dead" She stood, steadying herself on the frame of the cabana, and straightening her shoulders and pushing her sunglasses back on the bridge on her nose, walked over to the Surf Side.

22

Marty was washing glasses as she approached the bar and his face beamed to see her up and about. She sat down and asking for a bottle of water told him that soon her husband would be down for drinks and then she'd be off for a pedicure. Small talk, sips of water and casually asking if he was stocked for the busiest part of his day. They were leaving tomorrow she reminded, he should take advantage of her offer to help while he still had the chance. He stood for a moment, wet hands on his hips, head tilted to one side, contemplating taking her up on it and sizing up whether or not she looked like she would pass out while he was gone. Looking around at all that still needed to be accomplished before the afternoon rush, he squeezed her elbows, thanking her and assured her he'd be right back.

She wasted no time crossing the bar to the small refrigerator and opening it, grabbed a can of orange LIVED seltzer. The fridge was not as full as she was imagining it would be and she at this point just had to hope it was full enough and Marty was busy enough that he wouldn't notice an open can shoved in the back. The hiss it made when she popped it open reminded her of a snake and she thought for a split second how apropos that was. Her eyes concealed behind her sunglasses scanned the vicinity for any approaching guests as she reached into her pocket and felt for the baggie. Thrusting her hand inside, her fingers found the smooth pebble and paused. She took a deep breath and squeezed her eyes shut tight. Was she talking herself into it, or talking herself out of it? It was as if the Universe felt her waiver and sent a huge kick in the ass in the form of a baby's cry.

She opened her eyes and in the distance saw a father comforting his infant; walking and bouncing as the child's screeches turned into sobs. Without another thought, she pulled the round pellet out of her pocket and dropped it into the open mouth of the can expecting it to fizz, or overflow or something. Holy shit she'd seen too many movies. Holy shit, you're damn right she'd seen too many movies, and grabbing a dingy bar cloth, wiped off the outside of the can. Quickly she looked around for a second cloth, sure that Marty would be back any second, and covering her hand with it picked up the can and shoved it into the back of the fridge. A cloth in each hand she wiped any other cans she may have touched and closed the fridge, wiping as she went.

Marty paused at the entrance to the bar, his cart filled with supplies to see her wiping down the counters. Turning she saw him and smiled hoping for once that her sickness would come in handy and disguise her guilt. She put the rags down and wiping her hands on her cover up, adjusted her sunglasses and sat down at the bar. They chatted as he stocked the bar; she realized he'd only been gone for mere minutes and wondered when her husband would return. Again she mentioned their departure, and lamented about their return home and how difficult it would be to leave this place. He knew that she was not well, but she was certain he did not know to what extent. She kept the fact that she would never return to herself.

Her husband would be back soon she said. She would love to surprise him with this creation she used to drink back in her waitressing days. He promised to make her anything she asked for and she tapped her hands on her chin, pretending to remember the ingredients. The meds make her foggy she said whining a bit too much, but he didn't seem to notice. Guests came and went as he cut up fruit. She paid close attention to all the ingredients he used, wracking her brain for one that he didn't have available. She glanced at her phone, thinking that time must be at a stand still as her better half hadn't even been gone quite an hour yet. Looking up from her phone she saw him in the distance, weaving through the lounge chairs; the path he took having no rhyme nor reason.

Cherimoya!! She slammed her hand on the bar, startling Marty and halting his fruit cutting. It was Cherimoya they had used in the drink. He smiled and shook his head, sure he had never used it in any drink. The sweat started to drip down her back and she was all at once exhausted and lightheaded. Maybe the kitchen might have some she pressed, trying not to sound ridiculous and desperate; maybe they use it in those exotic meals they make. He laid the knife down and wiping his hands on those very same cloths that she had used to wipe away her guilt, said that only for her would he go check.

The adrenaline seemed to put her disease in remission and she was off the stool and behind the bar in one swift movement, nodding to him as he approached the bar. Even behind the sunglasses and that ridiculous floppy hat he looked confused to see her instead of the usual bartender. She smiled, explained that Marty had run to the kitchen and asked what he'd like, when of course she already knew. Willing herself not to open the fridge before he spoke, she waited for his response and tried to look unfamiliar with the bar's setup. He pointed to the fridge and standing between him and the refrigerator, she opened and leaned in front of it, blocking it's contents from his view. Reaching inside, she grabbed an unopened can and shaking it slightly opened it, fizzing and overflowing. In one fluid movement she put it down and grabbed the can that she had opened earlier, picked up a rag and turning towards him, pretended to wipe it off, while simultaneously kicking the door closed with her foot.

He shrugged his shoulders as she set the can on the bar, apologized for the mess and asked him if she could get him anything else. He shook his head from side to side and just like that there was no turning back. Goosebumps rose on her arms as she watched him walk away, once again weaving in and out amongst the beach chairs, without so much as a clue that he was holding in his hands the fate of the world. She reached in to the fridge and grabbing the opened can of seltzer, dumped it down the sink as she squeezed her eyes shut and took a deep breath. Pangs of guilt tore at her and she was overcome with waves of nausea as she thought about that poor secret service agent possibly getting blamed for this should it all go horribly wrong. As shaken as she was by the repercussions of her actions and the sheer magnitude of things that could go terribly awry on that seltzer's journey to it's intended target, she was at peace with whatever punishment she would receive for this, no matter the outcome. The Universe would bestow upon her what she deserved, one way or another, and if there was collateral damage here on earth, then the responsibility for it would lie squarely on her shoulders.

The adrenaline had worn off and left her weak and cognizant of just how sick she really was, as Marty entered the bar and saw it too. She had to lay down and at least try to get a little rest before he returned. from the suite. Marty's face was flushed with concern as he helped her back to the beach bed, and she was asleep before she was even fully horizontal.

23

When her eyes fluttered open he was smiling down at her with a mixture of concern and adoration, and seeing that she was awake, brushed the hair from her eyes. Her smile faded quickly as the memory of what she had done slammed her out of the hazy fog of sleep and back into reality. She quickly sat up and looked around the beach half expecting the world to be completely different than it had been an hour or so before, but her initial inspection found not one grain of sand out of place.

After spending a few minutes waking up and reassuring him that she was fine, they headed to the bar for a drink before her much anticipated pedicure. The kitchen hadn't had the Cherimoya that she had requested before she passed out, so Marty made them an original concoction that mimicked the distinctive flavor of the rare fruit, and they sipped them while waiting for her appointment time. Her eyes scanned the resort for any signs of the man in the floppy hat, or anyone acting out of the ordinary, reminding herself that the slow acting remedy that she had dispatched earlier was still at this point completely undetected.

He was acting funny; the way he did when he was planning something and when he dropped her off at the spa and kissed her, he said he'd be back in an hour. Her pedicure was very relaxing, and she was able to sip lemon water and almost completely fall asleep to sounds of running water and soft music. When he returned to pick her up, her tanned toes were the shade of brightly colored creamsicles and he handed her a freshly cut rose to match. They walked back to their room hand in hand, and although she could not seem to push the thoughts of what she had done out of her mind, she had to admit that at this moment she was feeling stronger than she had in days.

His hand slipped in front of her eyes as they entered their room, and when it was removed, hundreds and hundreds of roses met her gaze. A path carved through the sprawling suite led out to the balcony to a linen covered table set for two overlooking the ocean. Her arms encircled his neck and she kissed him hard as the tears rolled down her face at the thought of all the lies and omissions. She had never kept anything from him, and now she was keeping everything from him. The tears came faster when she thought of how he would feel knowing what she had done and how for the first time in their lives together, they hadn't been partners in crime. Luckily for her, she had so many things to cry about that guilt never crossed his mind and guilty tears looked and tasted just like tears filled with regret and sadness and fear.

As he dabbed at her face with the towel that hung around his neck, he told her that the night was full of possibilities, that he had amazing things planned, but first… they needed to have the conversation that they both were dreading. She told him she had to pee first; all that lemon water, and closed the door behind her as she sank onto the edge of the tub and covered her face with her hands. Get it out of your system she told herself; cry now. Act like you don't have the 411 on how different the world will look tomorrow. Make a plan, say yes to everything, pull yourself together. Have too much to drink for one of the last times in your life, forget what you've done, kiss him on that spot behind his ear that only you know and laugh like the world is coming to an end as you pray to the gods that it's not.

Standing up, she braced herself on the vanity, took a deep breath and stared at her reflection in a sort of silent pep talk. Slowly she nodded her head reassuring herself that one way or another all would be exactly as it should be, and for the very first time realized that she was the sacrifice. That was it, wasn't it? The master plan, the grand scheme, the Universe unfolding before her and never once until now did she realize that none of this was coincidence. Not her sickness, not her death, not her sharing a hotel with the DEVIL himself. She had never had control over any of it, and she smiled as the unexpected consciousness washed over her. She had fulfilled a destiny that she hadn't even been aware of until this very moment, and the tears she had tried so hard to stop, ran down her cheeks baptizing her in the peace she had been searching for since her diagnosis.

When she emerged from the bathroom, she had gotten her shit together and joined him in leaning against the railing of the balcony. She put her head on his shoulder and his arm encircled her waist, pulling her closer. They talked for more than an hour, she listened to his worries and fears and his plan to survive the next few months. He wanted to move the children back into the house, convinced that they needed to be together, to watch out for each other because they had no way of knowing what this new regime would do next. A woman with a terminal illness and a brand new baby made both families vulnerable, but together they would stand a better chance. He had been instructing the children to take out sums of money while they had been gone and they had opened overseas accounts to protect a good portion of their assets. The rest was hidden. The children had also been instructed to stockpile meds for her. Dr. Woodstock had been more than accommodating, and had even written her extra prescriptions. He was assuming that right now his job was secure, and working as much as possible would be beneficial in light of the future's uncertainty, another reason the kids living with them to help out was a good idea.

When it was over, he took a deep breath, and grasping her shoulders, kissed her first on the forehead, then on the lips, and told her to go check the bed. She smirked and headed into the bedroom to find a shiny purple frock lying there, paired with shoes to match. She wagged her finger at him and reached out to touch the silky smooth material. It was her favorite color, and she couldn't remember the last time she had really dressed up.

They showered and got dressed. She was slightly disturbed by how the dress even in a size 3 times smaller than she had worn most of her life hung a little too loosely. How desperate she had always been to lose weight, never thinking that the fulfillment of that wish would come with a hefty price. Still, she loved this dress and she felt beautiful for the first time in a very long time. There would never be another night like tonight. Ever. All the bad energy and what ifs needed to be forgotten if only for the next few hours.

Their last night in paradise before what seemed like the end of the world, and what was most definitely the end of her life, was spent with each other and no one else. Their dinner on the balcony watching the sunset was followed by a walk on the beach under the stars. They danced as he hummed their song and reminisced about memories that only two people in the whole world shared. She was giving them to him for safe keeping, to have and to hold until they were together again.

As tired as she was she kept going, soaking in every second of this time together. When thoughts of the day's events crept into her mind, she pushed them away before sheer panic set in. She fought the urge to keep track of time, trying desperately to live in the moment and not dwell on whether or not someone in another part of the resort had found the president dead. Being terminally ill was a great cover for stress and anxiety.

Returning to their room, talking and laughing in the dark turned into making love. She laid there for a long time, listening to him breathe, waiting for sleep to take her too, when she heard the first helicopter. Slipping out of bed, careful not to wake him, she peered out of the curtains to see a helicopter trying to land near the far side of the resort. How long would it take for them to come for her? How long before they traced the cause of death back to the seltzer and the unfamiliar woman behind the bar? With a dead president... she assumed not long at all. It was still two hours until daylight, and seven hours until checkout; maybe they could get home before they put two and two together. Of course though, they'd have a list of guests, they'd get her back at home too. She was kind of wishing that ANY of this had entered her mind before she impulsively decided to go all rogue superhero and save the world. Turning from the window she looked at him sleeping; blissfully unaware that hours before he had fucked a murderer. She wryly wondered if that had been on his bucket list and covering her mouth stifled a chuckle that became a sob.

A few deep breaths later and she was writing a note to leave on her side of the bed so that he wouldn't freak out when he awoke. She remembered heaving the sock under the armoire and gently lowered herself onto her knees to retrieve it. Reaching into her beach bag, her hand found the smooth bottle buried inside. Carefully she placed it under the dirty clothes in her side of the dresser and silently closed the drawer. There was no way that sleep would find her so she went out onto the balcony to watch the distant lights and wait for the sunrise.

24

The first hint of fiery orange crept over the horizon and she hugged her legs, resting her chin on her knees. She didn't notice her feet rubbing together nervously of their own volition, a habit usually reserved for the moments before she ran headlong into sleep. It had been a long time since she had seen any lights, and any sounds she might have heard had been carried out to sea or muffled by the crashing waves. The burning colors of the sky had been replaced with a muted palette of blues and lavenders as the sun fought the darkness to start another day. Cornflower and periwinkle formed a perfect gradient that could never be purposefully reproduced and for just that brief minute or two it was almost impossible to tell where the sea ended and the sky began. Then out of nowhere, there it was; breaking through the pastel sky and ending her very last night of anonymity. Surrounded by thin veils of clouds, it would take mere seconds to bloom fully from its hiding place beneath the horizon; mere seconds for the stillness to become daybreak and yet plenty of time for the whole world to change.

He walked out onto the balcony, hugging himself in the morning chill and squinting against the risen sun. She smiled at his scrunched up face and opened her arms for him to join her on the lounger. He straddled it behind her and she leaned beck onto his chest as his arms enveloped her. Just hours before she had been so conflicted, resolute and ashamed all in the same minute. Now she had come to a kind of peace within herself and looking out over the water she just knew that her destiny had been fulfilled.

They didn't hear the knock or the sheet of paper being slipped under the door, so when she saw him stoop to pick it up she was surprised at her serenity. He read the notice out loud to her. There had been a fire in a section of the resort undergoing renovations, and all departures were to be made from the North entrance. All guests were to expect delays and should plan on leaving earlier than usual to accommodate the crowds. He looked up at her and shrugged, satisfied with renovations on the south side of the hotel as the explanation for all of their speculation, and picked up the phone to order breakfast.

It was delivered as they finished packing, just as she needed to sit and rest. She was running on vapors at this point, having had no real sleep to speak of in almost 48 hours. There was no real appetite either but she knew that she would most likely be too weak to face anything that might be thrown at them on the journey home unless she at least ate something. She forced down a croissant and a little bit of yogurt, managing to sip some coffee while looking out over the sea one last time. Every time she thought she had grasped that concept; ONE LAST TIME, it flattened her again like a steamroller. It just seemed impossible; incomprehensible. One last deep breath and she stood up feebly; steadying herself for the trip home.

The bellmen came for their luggage and they went down to the veranda for one last look while they waited for their transport. He held her up as the emotions overtook her and the knowledge that she would never again stare out over the ocean became too much to bear. As she composed herself and wiped her eyes, she spotted it in the sand. She had found some beautiful treasures on the beach, but this; this was the perfect shell. She broke from his embrace and stepped off the veranda; the sand pouring between her feet and into her sandles. Smiling triumphantly, she raised it above her head, turning to show him. He clapped and smiled; the tears he'd managed to hold in until now flooding onto his cheeks. He held out his hand to her, signaling that it was time to go, and she reluctantly joined him on the stone patio, kicking the sand out of her shoes.

One last look.

One last hug.

One last kiss with the end of the earth as the backdrop to their love affair and they forgot for just a second what life was holding for them as they turned and stepped into the lobby.

When they finally boarded the oversized van that would take them to the airport, they were told to prepare themselves for long lines going through customs as new federal restrictions had been imposed that were making entering the country very difficult. Rubbing her eyes she thought that the guy on that microphone didn't know the half of it. She'd consider herself lucky not to be arrested or shot on sight before she even made it to her gate.

She sat on the suitcase hugging his legs as they waited in line after line; every one a new checkpoint. They checked their bags, their documents, their tickets. They questioned their visit, their citizenship, and asked ridiculous questions hoping to catch someone trying to illegally enter the country. When they finally were sitting on the plane and it backed out of the gate, she could hardly believe that she was on her way home. As the aircraft taxied down the runway, she was gripped by fear and panic, not for what she had done, but because in that minute she was sure she had gone completely mad and hallucinated the whole thing. Where was the news of his death? Where was the panic and chaos? By the time the plane's wheels left earth she had convinced herself that turning on the news at home would prove her insane as he paraded across the screen heralding the end of life as they knew it. She reached for his hand, bit her bottom lip and closed her eyes.

He didn't want to wake her; she had been so exhausted that she had just suddenly passed out, but it was time for her mid morning meds so he gently shook her awake. It was never really a surprise for her to be a bit disoriented upon awakening, so when she asked him as her eyes fluttered open if everything was still the same, he just smiled and handed her the capsules. He shook her awake again as they were landing and when she asked him if they knew what she had done, he kissed her forehead and patted her arm, happy that soon they would be in the fortress of their own home.

The children were there to meet them and their daughter in law had gone from barely looking pregnant to looking like they could have a grand baby any minute. They crowded around her, lavishing her with hugs and kisses, and she thought that she never wanted to let go. On the ride from the airport, he tried to bring up the imminent border closing but the kids kept changing the subject, insisting that the traffic warranted laser focus and that they would discuss everything that had happened in their absence when they arrived at home.

Their house looked like a castle to her as they pulled into the driveway. Almost 3 months of hotel rooms, no matter how large and roomy they had been, had left her forgetting just how spacious their home really was. She stood at the back door, surveying the yard, excited to see the green grass that had been so dry and brown when they had left. A fire would be lovely on a chilly spring night, she thought, but first…. she needed to see a TV. She folded her arms against a shiver as she walked into the family room to grab the remote and found eight sets of eyes staring at her as she hit the top step. He helped her to the couch and she looked from one to another trying to read in their faces exactly what was happening as she slowly perched on the edge of the sofa and folded her hands in her lap.

He was smiling then; on his knees in front of her and kissing her hands as tears dotted his cheeks and he was grinning. Her confusion was not an act as she wondered out loud what was going on. Their daughter was wiping away tears as she cried on the dog, and her son was hugging his wife. She shook her head feeling for a second that everything was happening in slow motion. She saw his lips moving but couldn't hear any words and as he hugged her he pressed his damp cheek against hers and whispered in her ear.

He's dead.

The look of disbelief on her face caused him to reach for the remote and turn on the television; it didn't matter what channel. The BREAKING NEWS graphic was on every station and the morbid celebrations that had broken out all over the country were splashed across the screen. She heard herself ask who had done it and as if on cue the scrolling news ribbon read "apparent heart attack". She was numb. Not sad or scared or relieved or sorry…. just numb. On what seemed like autopilot she made her way to the kitchen. Her feet were like cinderblocks that at the same time seemed to float above the floor. She poured herself a glass of bourbon; a really large glass of bourbon. The glass was empty before anyone could even attempt to wrangle it out of her hands and she figured that it would help whatever this numb thing was last until she could pass out in that king sized bed.

He practically carried her up the stairs and she laid there a long time after he had slipped off his side of the bed and out the door. Not for one second did she believe this was over. There would be autopsies and a lengthy investigation. The best she could hope for was that she would die first so that this poor man she had left in the dark and her doctor couldn't be implicated. Her brain was reeling from the booze, and she knew that tomorrow would bring more information; good or bad so she let herself drift off into unconsciousness and hoped the buzz would be strong enough to squelch any dreams.

He descended the stairs and joined them on the couch as they continued to sit mesmerized by the news coverage. He was relieved that she had passed out. She had seemed so confused and disoriented, he assumed from a long travel day and this overwhelming chain of events. He would cuddle up next to her shortly, but right now he wasn't even a bit ashamed to be reveling in another man's death. He looked at his children and for the first time in almost a decade he believed that they were free. The thought that his grandchild would be brought into this world free made the hairs on his arms stand at attention.

26

Not one dream. Staring at the ceiling she couldn't recall one dream. The sun was bright and her head was heavy as she reached for the glass of water on her nightstand. The first five was reading her the riot act and she knew that the only news she would be watching today would be seen from the vantage point she held at this very moment. Opening the pill bottle was a struggle, hoisting her body up on one arm was next to impossible even with all the weight she had lost. She had seen the way the kids looked at her when she stepped off the plane, wanting so badly to squeeze her and so frightened that she would break. She knew it was coming, she almost wondered if the Universe was just waiting; giving her strength to do what she was made for and now was telling her that time was up. She needed to have a talk with that Universe though, because it owed her one. It owed her a grandchild.

The door opened as she turned on the TV, and he and the old lady baby joined her on the bed. If the dog got any closer, they'd have been wearing the same clothes; it was as if she too knew that the clock was winding down. The news couldn't really tell them anything earth shattering. He had died from what appeared to be a massive heart attack at an undisclosed location. His body had landed overnight and had been driven amidst the thousands of people partying through the streets of the Capital to his residence where he would lie in state. There was as of yet no discussion of an autopsy, they would not reveal where he died, and the Madame Secretary had been sworn in within minutes of learning of his death. As long as she stayed alive, the elections would go on as planned and democracy would be protected.

The death of the president did not wrap the world up in the neat little bow that she had envisioned. In the weeks that followed, the country was thrown into turmoil and the initial joy and celebration was replaced by fear, apprehension and political upheaval as the opposition tried to carry out the work that their master had begun. The newly sworn in President was practically covered in bubble wrap and squirreled away to keep from being assassinated, and there were riots and cells of violence in multiple cities daily. It was not an easy road back from the climate he had created. A week or so after their return, a LIVED employee had leaked the name of the resort that the president and his entourage had been holed up in. It had never been confirmed nor denied, and the government swore up and down that there was still an investigation underway. It seemed highly likely that an investigation would turn up nothing as even his own party didn't care much what had killed him. She thought she should tell him then while he was still shocked and reeling from the news that they had been vacationing mere yards away from him at the moment of his demise. She only needed to show him the missing pellet and he would be convinced. Would that make him an accessory? She thought it very probably might and also thought as she watched the twin to her weapon of choice circle the toilet bowl and disappear, that watching his wife die before his very eyes was enough of a burden to carry for one lifetime.

She had hoped in her last few days on the earth she would watch the country she loved come back from the brink. In fact, she just may have traded her soul for it. As the weeks wore on, she barely left her bed. People came to visit and no matter how much she hated having anyone see her in her current (and final) state, she knew that very soon there would come a time when she would no longer be conscious. The children came every single day and no matter how exhausted she was she stayed awake long enough to feel that baby kick. She suspected that she would slip away immediately following holding her grandchild in her arms and looking into those newly opened eyes.

He had gone back to work almost ceremoniously, as it had only lasted a few weeks and he had almost immediately taken the leave of absence that he had been planning. Funeral arrangements were in place and she had made her wishes known to both him and the children. There was to be no open casket. She wanted a plain and simple pine box and to be cremated; her ashes scattered with his when the time came. She wanted a party, with drinking and laughter and speeches where people said really nice shit and told their favorite stories about her. She had even left instructions for what was to occur when it came time for her to go. She had chosen a song that would usher her from this life to the next surrounded by the faces that her soul would take along with it on the trip.

Her son and daughter had converted the large upstairs guest room into a home birthing space and temporary nursery once they realized she would not be able to leave the house to go to the hospital, assuring that she could be present for the birth and hold her grandchild right away. It seemed that there was nothing left to do but wait.

27

One afternoon, he walked into their room, sat on the bed, and brushing her hair from her eyes announced that Dr. Woodstock was downstairs. Her heart leapt and a thin smile crept across her lips as she told him to bring her up. A few minutes later the good doctor was standing before her and she weakly patted the bed, inviting her to get closer. He closed the door behind him, leaving them alone to talk and to say goodbye. The corners of the doctor's eyes were wet and she smiled as she made small talk, asking about their time away and if she had heard the rumor about the president dying there. Yes she had heard but did not elaborate. They chatted about the trips, and the arrival of the baby and finally got around to the hard stuff.

Finally the doctor just asked point blank if she was ready to go and if she wanted to use the option she had been given. She wasn't sure why she answered the way that she did. No one would ever have to know. She could slip out of this world; her sins or virtues undetected, and no one would be the worse for wear. Maybe she was looking for absolution at the eleventh hour, or to unload her baggage, or maybe she just didn't want to be alone in this anymore. Whatever the reason, she told the doctor that the pellets were gone. The doctor cocked her head to the side and squinting one eye grimaced and asked if she had taken both. Looking the doctor right in the eye slowly she swung her head from side to side. She explained that one had been used and that she had made the decision to take her husband's options away by flushing the other.

The doctor shook her head as if that would help her to better understand, and staring into her eyes repeated that one had been used? No further words needed to be spoken as the realization washed over her. The doctor removed her glasses leaving them to dangle from her neck as she rubbed her eyes. Unsure of how she felt, she could only bite her lip and look at the dying woman before her. She could not lie. She was happy and relieved that he was gone, but was ambivalent about the part that she had played in his death. She could not crucify her patient for her actions and yet as one who had sworn to first do no harm, she also could not celebrate them. They talked about how she had kept the secret until now and had never expected to burden anyone with it and how as relieved as she was, she was also sorry that she had burdened her. The choice of what to do with the information that she had been given was hers to make. The doctor, holding her hand in hers assured her that when her suffering was over here, there would not be any left behind; she could go peacefully with the knowledge that her family would be safe.

They parted for the very last time amidst both tears and smiles, the doctor hugging a frail frame that was once strong and vital. They had no doubt that they would see each other on the other side, especially now that they shared a secret that would forever connect them. She watched as the doctor tried to keep her composure as she left the room, but could hear the sobs as she closed the door behind her. The time that they had spent together had exhausted her and with her soul feeling lighter than it had in weeks, she immediately fell fast asleep.

Dusk had shrouded the room in a purplish hue and opening her eyes she could see him sitting in that yard sale chair hugging that perfect pillow and watching her sleep. In the dimness that hung over the room he couldn't see that she was awake and she watched him roll the corner of the pillow between his first and middle fingers absentmindedly as he had done since he was a little boy. He brushed the corner of the fabric across his lips and wiped his eyes as she purposely started to stir to give him time to compose himself. She was so tired of fighting, and she was so ready to go that she was sure, without a shred of doubt that end game was much harder for him than it was for her. In one fluid movement he was off the chair and climbing gingerly onto the bed to get as close to her as possible. He wanted her to try and eat even though he knew her answer was always the same. She appeased him by agreeing to a cup of broth; nothing too thick or lumpy, and he smiled knowing deep inside that sipping on a cup of broth changed nothing. He had some things that he needed to tell her. Things that would speed up the inevitable and he was stalling.

When he returned with the bowl of broth, she was dozing and the sound of the tray being placed on the dresser roused her from her twilight sleep. He helped her to sit up, adjusted her pillows behind her and rolled up the sleeves of her oversized sweatshirt. Everything was oversized now, and because she was always cold, the only time she wasn't wearing a sweater or sweatshirt was when he helped her bathe. Sipping slowly, the warm broth hit her empty stomach and she fought to keep it down. He was there with the napkin, wiping her chin and pushing her hair out of her eyes. She thought then what a child she had become. How she never again would do anything for herself and what this ghastly end to her life might be like had she not had him to wipe her mouth… and her ass. Feebly raising the spoon to her lips, she smiled at him thinly, wishing it could be the biggest smile he had ever seen and not needing a mirror to know that it was not.

It only took a few spoonfuls for her to have had enough. She waved the spoon away, laid back on the pillows and closed her eyes wincing in pain as he took the tray off the bed and set it back on the dresser. Crawling across the bed on his hands and knees, he got a chill seeing how tiny she looked under the covers and gently curled up next to her, thankful that since she had learned of the monster's demise, the nightmares had ceased. Once again he rolled their decisions over and over in his mind. They had decided against any care with the exception of Dr. Woodstock's homeopathic treatments and he had promised to abide by her wishes, but on days like this, it was unbearable to watch her suffer. He hadn't broached the subject of the tiny pellets they had hidden away, at least not yet. There would come a time that he would offer them to her against his better judgment, but he would nonetheless, knowing that it was her decision and her decision alone to end this nightmare. Hearing the breath that used to lull him to sleep, now slow and labored, he decided to wait to tell her the news until tomorrow morning. He closed his eyes and once again hoped that there would be a tomorrow.

Steam curled up from his coffee mug as he stood in the kitchen staring out into the backyard. The grass was dappled in sunlight and the dew glistened, signaling the start of another beautiful summer day. He had been up for hours, first lying in the darkness listening to her breathe, and then slipping silently out of their bed and sitting in the family room. The glow of the streetlights fell on the pictures that told the story of their history together, as he listened to the silence and tried to figure out how to tell her. What in most lives would be a beginning, these words would herald the end.

Now as he looked out over the property they had built their lives on, he thought that maybe one last fire on a summer night might be just the way. He smiled when he thought of all of the times she would have a little too much bourbon and get dramatic and sentimental about the dying fire. Those very last embers so often brought her to drunken tears. She would lament how she didn't want the night to end, every time like it was the last fire they would ever build, like it was the last time they would ever have those hours together, just the two of them.

She hated endings.

Especially when they didn't go exactly how she had pictured them.

The bedroom door opened and she saw him peek through the crack to see if she was awake. The first five had pretty much fallen by the wayside when feeling shitty every minute of every day had taken over, but this morning she didn't seem to be in as much pain upon awakening as she had for the last couple of weeks. She managed a thin smile when she saw one brown eye staring at her from the hallway and he smiled back as he entered the room. Kicking off his slippers, he joined her on the bed and kissing her forehead proposed his idea for a fire. That familiar feeling returned, the one that she gotten so used to feeling since she realized everything she did was for the last time. It was sort of a sadness mixed with consternation that turned into acquiescence as she remembered that there wasn't thing fucking one she could do about this. Cupping his cheek in her hand she smiled and nodded at the plan, and hoped there would be bourbon.

He turned on reruns of her favorite old show; she had been sleeping so much that she had hardly noticed that the news channels had been visibly absent from the TV. The truth was, she didn't care. It felt like a dream to her; a delusion. Sometimes she had to ask him to show her pictures of their vacation when she had convinced herself that that too had never happened. At this late in the game, if they were going to come for her, they would have come and she could not say for certain whether what she had done had saved the world or sent it further into a spiraling descent toward certain obliteration. All day she laid there, watching reruns, drifting in and out of sleep and waiting for nightfall.

He left her sleeping and went out to prepare the yard for their last fire. It had been a long time since they had made use of the fire pit and it was full of ash and charred wood. He stood there for a long time remembering the day she had built it. Looking at the driveway he saw her as clear as day pulling in, all proud of herself with everything she needed piled in the back of the SUV. Together they had worked on it all day. He had never seen her beaming with such pride at an accomplishment before. He chuckled and shook his head at the memory; grateful that looking back could still spark happiness, and hopeful that it always would.

Things were pretty much in order by dusk. He had cleaned all the chairs and even brought out a chaise lounger for her to lay on. Wood was stacked neatly and he had gone down the road to collect the kindling; something she had always loved to do with the kids. He had the wood in the fire pit all ready to be lit and staring at it with his hands on his hips he spontaneously began to cry. He wept long and hard, his tears falling in large drops, splattering on the dry patio paving stones. Leaning over, he braced himself on his knees and let the emotion overtake him, praying that this was his soul's way of purging now so that he didn't come unglued later. Heaving almost to the point of throwing up, he finally regained control of himself and wiping his nose with the back of his hand, slowly straightened up and looked up at their bedroom window and the setting sun reflecting in it. He took a deep breath and thought that it was time to go and wake his love.

29

She had been awake for about a half hour and had even managed to make it to the bathroom by herself when he entered the bedroom wearing the most forced smile she had ever seen. Her eyes followed him as he crossed the room to her dresser and rifled through her clothes finding something warmer for her to wear. Selecting a pair of heavy sweatpants and a silky soft long sleeve shirt he laid them on the bed and went into his closet to retrieve one of his oversized heavy cardigans for her to wear overtop. She pushed aside the covers and he helped her dress, completing her ensemble by pulling on the pair of heavy socks her brother had given her before their trip. No shoes required as she hadn't descended the stairs in a month and he was hoping that those socks would be removed so that she could warm her toes by the fire.

Light as a feather he thought as he carried her down the stairs to the lounger that he had padded with blankets and placed in front of the fire pit.

One strike of a match was all it took to set the dry kindling ablaze, and sitting back he looked at her profile in the firelight and it was like cramming his heart in a vise. Reaching for her hand to grab her attention, he put up one finger, smiled and from behind his lounge chair pulled a bottle of their favorite bourbon and 2 glasses. She pulled his cardigan around her tighter and smiled as he served them each a hefty pour and turned on the music. They had fire music; music that made the world fall away. They might as well have been in the middle of a forest primeval instead of their backyard as long as they were together and had their fire, their booze and their music.

When she was halfway through her glass he thought he should spill his guts. He was in a precarious spot of supplying enough alcohol to take the edge off the news, but needing her to be sober enough to process the information. At this point neither of them gave much thought to drinking in her condition, the here and the now was all that mattered. Alcohol could neither help nor hinder what was quickly approaching, and enjoyment and comfort were reasons enough now to do just about anything. Placing his glass on the table between them, he perched on the edge of her lounge chair and took her hand in his. Good news he thought shouldn't be preceded by such apprehension and dread, and yet here he was filled with both.

They had never had a conversation about what would cause her to finally let go. They didn't have to. She had always wanted to be a grandmother; it was her dream and so he led with that news first, knowing that just speaking the words was enough to put the end in motion. When he was finished telling her about how their daughter in law's doctors had chosen to induce her by the end of the week, and how they had told them most likely just knowing she would be induced would send her into labor, he took a deep breath and kissed her forehead. She smiled up at him, letting it sink in. The unknown was no longer a mystery. She had a week at most left on this earth and one of her favorite lyrics jumped to mind reminding her that we are all temporary, and a slow and labored sigh slipped from her lips.

Not that anything could lighten the mood after basically giving someone their death date, but he thought he could at least try to give her some peace if nothing else. He hoped the next words that came out of his mouth would cut through the tension that hung heavier over them now than the smoke that poured from the fire pit. Picking up his glass, he lightly clinked hers and he explained to her how every criminal who had been involved in planning the coup had been tracked down and was now in prison awaiting what was sure to be an endless stream of trials. He touched her glass with his again, took a sip and revealed that the candidate that had supposedly been selected to "succeed" HIM had been among those arrested and with no candidate to run against Madame Secretary in the elections, she would automatically become the next President; an election would be nothing but a formality. A heart attack he went on, had very possibly saved the world.

There was no way to keep her hand steady as she brought the glass to her lips, and no way in the glow of the fire to hide the tears that followed each other's tracks down her thin, pale face. It was good news, but it was also the last nail in that pine box she had requested. It was confirmation that her destiny had been fulfilled and the birth of that baby was her cue to exit stage left. The tears slowly falling onto his cardigan were composed of both relief and sadness, and the salt made her want more bourbon as she resolutely polished off what was left in her glass.

Hours later they had burned every piece of wood and the dying embers signaled the end of her very last fire. This time though she was unwavering in the face of the finality of it all. She had spent all of the tears on herself and there were none left to mourn the fire. She sipped what was left in her glass as he poured water over the hot, bright embers and feeling good and drunk hoped that they had bourbon wherever she was going. The water hit the fire with a sound that reminded her of sizzling steak and the steam and smoke that billowed up from the pit disappeared among the trees and stars. Satisfied that the fire was out, he carried her upstairs and helped her change her clothes and climb into bed. The decrease in her body weight had caused her to be much more inebriated than she would have been in the past and she fell asleep so fast that she never heard him say I love you. He curled up next to her and shared her pillow, smelling the smoke that still clung to her hair.

30

She woke up every morning in an immense amount of pain, so the fogginess that accompanied this morning's suckfest had almost gotten lost in her failed attempts not to cry. She couldn't remember the last time she had been hungover, but for the rest of her life she'd remember the last. Every movement brought her to tears and she reached for her phone to text him and almost passed out from the pain. His footsteps running up the stairs meant that relief was on the way and that she could try to unclench the fists that were glued to her sides as the pain seized her. Almost immediately he was beside her, soothing her and lifting her head as he firmly pushed the pills through her lips. A towel was held to her chin, as experience had taught him that only some of the water would make it into her mouth until the pain eased up and she could take sips on her own. The time that it took for the pain to loosen it's grip had increased exponentially in the last weeks and he was giving her more and more meds in an attempt to keep her comfortable and failing miserably.

They had decided that she should call her family and that they should come and say their goodbyes in the next day or two. At her insistence, none of them had seen her since before they had left on their vacation. In fact, with the exception of Dr. Woodstock, she had refused visits from anyone after the first few weeks that they were back, but she knew now that it was time. After many tear filled conversations about what she believed would happen when she drew her last breath, he knew that there was no question in her mind that she would be with all of them for always. She didn't feel like this was goodbye; but just see you later, and the goodbyes were not for her sake, but for everyone else's. Still, they deserved closure as much as she deserved to believe that death was not the end of anything; just a continuation of what she started here with all of the people that she loved, so of course she would suffer the goodbyes.

Two days later, she had gotten through another dreadful pain filled morning knowing that the afternoon would be spent with her brothers and sisters. She was the baby of the family and their parents had both passed away before she had even gotten married. Her oldest brother had stood in for her dad; walking her down the aisle and they had always been so close it was like they had been separated at birth. She loved all of her siblings, they were all such different people and they had often had their differences, but she loved each one of them for different reasons. She laid in her bed waiting for them to arrive and wondered what they would say if they knew what she had done. Would her sisters turn her in? Would her brothers thank her? She thought most likely that if she blurted it out during their visit, they would all think she was hallucinating or recounting a horrible dream. There were days she wasn't sure that she wasn't doing both.

He was choosing something for her to wear for their visit, having given her a bath the night before and washing her hair. The kids were here to see their aunts and uncles and her daughter had fixed her hair as best she could. She expected that there wasn't a way to make her look like she wasn't dying. She was grateful for the effort, but counting the minutes until she could just close her eyes and hoping she didn't pass out mid sentence and scare the shit out of everyone. Maybe, she wondered out loud as he looked up from her dresser drawers, he should brief them before their audience with the breathing corpse. With a deep, long sigh he agreed and told her not to worry about one more thing. He would take care of it. He knew how anxious she had become about the baby's birth; knowing that if induction was necessary, it would all occur at the hospital, which may as well be a million miles away. There wasn't really anything left in Dr. Woodstock's arsenal to give her so he was trying to keep her as calm as possible. As if on cue, the doorbell rang. Her daughter helped her get dressed, while he went downstairs to let in her family.

One at a time they entered her room, hoping that their awkward smiles would be a big enough distraction from the eyes that had been wiped and rewiped. There were a lot of confessions and I'm sorries; but just as many laughs and I love yous. Visiting with her oldest brother and his wife ended the gauntlet and the grief she felt knowing that she would never look into his eyes again surprised and overwhelmed her. After hours spent comforting those that loved her with a promise that this wasn't goodbye, watching him walk out the door left her engulfed in sadness and as her husband held her tight, she cried almost to the point of unconsciousness. It took lots of time, lots of pills and a panicked phone call to their favorite doctor for advice to calm her down and finally get her to sleep. With everything he had been through in the last eight months, he had never been so completely and viscerally exhausted, and passing out next to her, he slept through until morning for the first time since last fall.

31

He awoke to his son gently but firmly shaking him awake. Realizing that he was still fully clothed and on top of the covers, he immediately felt that something was wrong. He looked to his left and breathed a sigh of relief seeing that she was still sleeping soundly. Still, his son was standing above him and the look on his face said that ready or not his day was up and running. They talked in the hallway as not to wake her and the look on his son's face plucked at his heartstrings, because he remembered seeing that very same look in the mirror the day before he was born. She had just started having contractions an hour or so ago and they had contacted the midwife who was on her way to examine her. There was no reason to believe that this would be happening immediately since the contractions were still fifteen minutes or so apart and her water had not broken. Still though, he needed to wake the soon to be grandmother and get some meds into her so that they could get a jump on managing the pain. It was going to be another long and stressful day, but he dreaded the day that was coming when the stress would be replaced with nothing at all.

The midwife arrived and after her initial examination concluded that their daughter in law hadn't begun to dilate yet and instructed them to keep timing the contractions. They had learned all of the tools to keep her comfortable and to work through them and she would return when they started coming a little closer together.

As his daughter in law's labor progressed, he stayed upstairs with his wife all day, watching TV and holding her hand. It was so comforting to have their family together under one roof for such a momentous occasion; with updates only a few feet away. There was no talk of what came next. For now they were just a couple eagerly awaiting their first grandchild, even if one of them was expending all of her energy just trying to stay conscious.

Maybe she could hang on, she thought, despite her every movement causing excruciating pain. She wanted to cry at the thought but after yesterday had neither the energy nor the tears. The fight was all but gone. She was given a purpose, and now she would stay just long enough to savor the reward. Her body was so very tired. Hour by hour she willed herself to stay on this plane, in this dimension, even as her soul pulled on her to just fall away. Would she meet him there she wondered? Had she been righteous? Would she have made the same choice if she hadn't already known how her story would end? She believed now that her purpose had been revealed to her after the fact. Or had it just been the justification a dying woman had created and convinced herself of? It wouldn't be long now before she would know all of the answers to EVERYTHING. If only she could share them with her babies and her love.

When the midwife finally came back it was almost midnight. She had long since been asleep, and he was shifting back and forth between joining his daughter pacing in the hallway waiting for updates and lying on the bed watching her sleep. He thought about this time tomorrow night and how watching her like this might be a very different experience. He had portrayed the strong future widower in the numerous talks that he had had with the children and with her siblings. A grieving husband displaying confidence that she would be with him forever; that this was just a rest stop on their journey towards the same destination and he would meet her when his job was done here. The truth was though, all that confidence was for their benefit. He was scared shitless that he'd never feel her again. Every time it occurred to him that maybe she had made all of that up for HER benefit, his knees buckled and forever without her loomed in front of him like a vast endless ocean waiting to swallow him whole.

He dozed for an hour or two, only to wake with a start and wonder how close he was to having a grandbaby. He could see faint light seeping through the blinds and he knew from all of his sleepless nights that sunrise was still an hour or so away. Rubbing his eyes he padded down the dimly lit hallway and put his ear to the guest room hoping to hear anything that might tell him what was happening. He knocked softly and a few seconds later his son opened the door and stepped into the hallway. It shouldn't be long now, she was nine centimeters dilated and everything was progressing just as it should be. He hugged his boy and patting him on the back told him that he would wake his mom and prepare her for the introduction she'd been waiting for. He left him to slip back into the room as he tiptoed down the stairs to make himself a cup of coffee.

A few minutes later he was sitting on the edge of the bed, rousing her gently armed with her morning pills and water. The coffee she loved so much had stopped being palatable about a month ago. Even the smell of it made her nauseous, as did almost every strong smell. He was barely able to get the bone broth down her once a day, and she had withered away to practically nothing. Her eyes fluttered open and then closed again and it was a full twenty minutes before she was fully awake and he could get the pills into her. She managed a weak smile when he told her the news and he cupped her chin and kissed her forehead in return. He had bathed her yesterday and his daughter had helped change the sheets and clean up the room a bit so that the baby could be brought in later in the day. Every time he thought he was playing a waiting game, it became obvious that the real one had yet to begin.

It was late morning when word came from down the hall that their daughter in law had begun to push. He had started to wear a hole in the hall rug and their daughter was beside her on the bed. The news had brightened her up a bit and she was so relieved and so happy for so many different reasons. Together they could hear the grunting and muffled yells of a woman in the last stages of labor and immediately she was thrust back into the delivery room the day that her own first child was born. She could feel her husband holding her hand and pressing his cheek to hers; whispering into her ear that she could do it and that he was so proud of her. She reached for her daughter's hand and smiled thinking of her birth as well and the tears he had shed knowing that they had somehow gotten one of each. Her little boy beaming as he held his baby sister... It had been the beginning of what she always referred to as "We Four". Her daughter reached to hug her when she saw her start to tear up and just then he burst into the bedroom to announce IT'S A GIRL! They had a granddaughter and for once, the tears they cried were there to wash away the thoughts of death and of loss. For right then, there was a new smell in the house and a reason to smile and to feel joy again. He sat on the edge of the bed and gently slid his arms under her back and held her to him, dampening her freshly washed hair with his tears, and somehow through all they had been through, he had never felt closer to her in his life.

While her son and his wife spent the first few hours of their new daughter's life getting to know every inch of her body and marveling at what they had made, she took more pills and slept. She did not want the birth of her granddaughter to revolve around her. They had already made so many concessions based on her circumstances, she wanted them to have the time that any other set of new parents without someone dying in the next room would have. Besides, she positively had not one ounce of energy left in her body, and although recharging for her was the understatement of the century, she needed whatever the drugs and sleep would provide. That little girl would be in her arms soon enough.

33

The moments that comprised the end of her life had landed in two categories: falling asleep and waking up. She was always doing either and there seemed to be nothing in between. She could no longer eat and she was pretty sure her secondary cause of death would be listed as starvation, but her brain worked just fine. There were moments when she wasn't positive that that was a good thing, because waking up from her latest nap, if you could call half of her existence a nap, her mind was racing. What she'd seen, what she'd done, where she was going. Part of her was actually excited to know the answers to the things she had questioned all of her life, but part of her just wanted to hang on. She knew that only one of those options was possible, so she tried to quiet her mind with the meditation she had been practicing for months and exist in the present, because she was going to meet her granddaughter.

The bedroom took on the solemnity of a church as her son and daughter in law entered carrying a pink bundle. He helped her sit up as best she could and fixed her pillows to help keep her upright and then crawled onto the bed next to her to assist if need be. Her daughter was taking a video of the momentous occasion and her daughter in law still in her bathrobe sat in the yard sale chair as her son leaned over and placed the sleeping infant into his mother's already cradled arms. The tears flowed and he dabbed at her eyes and then his and kissed the top of his granddaughter's head. Staring down at a perfect face surrounded in swaddling, she couldn't help but compare it to everyone in the room and ponder who this little miracle resembled. She kissed her forehead and closing her eyes, breathed deeply the smell of brand new life. The baby's eyes fluttered open and as their souls met through their first gaze into each other's eyes, her tiny lips parted in their first smile and it was like the room was flooded with the most amazing bright light that she had ever seen. Her husband asked if they had picked a name and the room grew silent as the new parents looked at each other.

They had decided to name her after her grandmother. Her husband became almost inconsolable as he crossed the room to hug first his son and then his daughter in law, but she just let the tears gently fall onto the fuzzy pink blanket and never broke that gaze. Her middle name was to be after the first female president because those two names were the first step to ensuring that she would grow up to be strong and kind and compassionate. Meeting her son's eyes she smiled, her arms had grown tired even supported on a pillow and she nodded to him that it was time to take his daughter back to the nursery. Her son stooped to take the baby and kissed her, followed by a kiss from her daughter in law whose hormones were barely allowing her to keep it together. She watched the family leave the room and only then allowed herself to crumble. Her daughter stopped recording, and crying followed her brother out the door.

He rocked her and shushed her as he held her. He knew she would be asleep in a matter of minutes, so he wiped her nose and gave her more pills and laid her down; fixing her covers and brushing her thinning hair from her eyes. She was out before the tears could even dry on her face, and he too was spent but he needed to make some phones calls before he could rest alongside of her.

The next few days were a quick decline. She was barely awake long enough to hold the baby but for a few minutes at a time and finally could not manage to hold her at all, so they placed her in the middle of the bed next to her. The only thing she could manage to pass her lips were pills and meager sips of water and it finally came to a point where even that was no longer feasible. Three days after the baby's arrival, he was lying on the bed as close to her as he could manage when she whispered that she couldn't hold on. The words pierced his heart as if it were a total surprise. He wanted to tell her not to go, that he needed her, that the baby needed her, that he could not do this life without her, that he couldn't remember how life existed before her and that the world would turn cold without her. Instead he just buried his face in her pillow; in her hair and wept. His love was ready to start the next adventure, and stopping her would be the selfish act of a grieving man. So instead he asked her if she wanted to use the doctor's gift, and watched as she shook her head from side to side.

They gathered in the master bedroom, talking as if she were participating in the conversation. Regaling family stories and laughing through the tears as they recounted one instance after another that only their family and their family alone would understand. She was in and out of consciousness and if she heard them speaking, she did not respond. They spent hours with her, only leaving to take turns feeding or changing their newest member and he could not help but check every so often to make sure that she was breathing.

It was dusk and they had lit candles instead of turning on the bright lights that she had always read by at bedtime. Her breath had become more labored and he sat by her side holding her hand and refusing to let go. Her eyes fluttered open and she was trying in the dim light to look around the room as they all moved closer so that she would know that they were with her.

She could see "we four" plus two crowded around her side of the bed, and her dog was pushed up against her, happy to be back on the bed after being relegated to the guest room with her daughter for weeks. She felt her hand in his and she knew like she had never known anything in her whole life, that it was time. It was barely a whisper but she knew by the muffled sounds of crying that they heard her say "I Love You" and that she would always be by their side. She squeezed his hand, and as he put his ear to her lips, she told him the pellets were gone. She had gotten rid of them and she wasn't sorry. His children and grandchildren needed him here. They would meet when his work was done. This was her time and he would have his. She said that she loved him; that she would never leave him and that it was time to put on her song, as she kissed him on the cheek. She could hear the lyrics to HOME playing and feel herself being pulled away as his tears fell on her face and his lips met hers for the last time…

Exit….stage left.

Made in the USA
Middletown, DE
20 December 2019